Nothing to hide?

"How about this boy?" The colonel grabbed me and gave me another teeth-rattling shake. "What the devil is Jesse Sherman doing here?"

Athena's face softened. Turning to the judge, she said, "Oh, sir, that poor child showed up this evening, begging at the back door. I fed him a few scraps and let him shelter by the fire. I didn't think you'd mind, sir."

The colonel cursed. "That's a damnable lie. I left the rascal for dead in the street at least three weeks ago. You been caring for him all this while, aiding and abetting him to steal the widow's slave child."

"Please let us search this house, Horatio," Mr. Kirby put in. "Henrietta is beside herself, she loves the child so."

I wanted to call the man a liar, but, if I spoke up, they'd all know that I'd seen Perry. So, like Athena, I kept my mouth shut.

The judge sighed heavily and headed for the cellar door. "Come with me," he said to the men. "You'll soon see I have nothing to hide."

The moment the judge's back was turned, Colonel Botfield grabbed my arm and twisted it pretty near out of the socket. "No matter how this little scene plays out," he whispered, "you ain't seen the last of me, Jesse Sherman. As sure as the sun rises in the east and sets in the west, I'll be your death, boy."

OTHER NOVELS BY MARY DOWNING HAHN

PROMISES
to the
DEAD

BY MARY DOWNING HAHN

🐦 sandpiper

Houghton Mifflin Harcourt

Boston New York

The text of this book is set in 12-point Goudy.

The Library of Congress has cataloged the hardcover edition as follows:
Hahn, Mary Downing.
Promises to the dead / by Mary Downing Hahn.
p. cm.
Summary: Twelve-year-old Jesse leaves his home on Maryland's
Eastern Shore to help a young runaway slave find a safe haven
in the early days of the Civil War.
[1. Slavery—Fiction. 2. Fugitive slaves—Fiction. 3. Afro-Americans—Fiction.
4. Orphans—Fiction. 5. United States—History—Civil War, 1861–1865—
Fiction. 6. Maryland—Fiction.] I. Title.
PZ7.H1256 Pr2000
[Fic]-dc21 99-048525
ISBN: 978-0-395-96394-4
ISBN: 978-0-547-25838-6 pb

Manufactured in the United States of America
EB 10 9 8 7 6 5 4 3 2 1

To the memory of Corporal Thomas N. Sherwood, 1st Regiment Infantry, Company B, Maryland Volunteers, and Private Charles W. Sherwood, Purnell Legion Infantry, Company A, Maryland Volunteers

CHAPTER 1

If my great-uncle Philemon hadn't gotten a sudden hankering for turtle soup, the story I'm about to tell would have come out different. Or maybe it wouldn't have happened at all. But then who's to speak with any certainty about what might or might not have been? Everyone knows fate has a way of finding us no matter how well hid we may think we are.

All I can say is my particular story started when my great-uncle decided a bowl of Delia's soup was just the thing for his rheumatism, which was fearsome bad in damp weather. Since the old man couldn't go hunting himself, not with his stiff knees and aching back, he sent me to the marsh instead. A little spring rain wouldn't hurt a boy my age, he said. Nor the wind either.

Delia raised her eyebrows at this and said, "Age got nothing to do with it. I never knew pneumonia to spare a body, young or old." But she didn't waste her breath arguing. Once my uncle got an idea in his head, nobody could shake it loose. Not even Delia, who had more sense than me and him put together.

Uncle Philemon gave her a vexed look and said nothing. Delia was the only slave he owned, and he treated her good most of the time, fearing she might run away if he didn't. He'd told her more than once he planned to free her when he died; it was already written in his will, item two, right after the part where he left me, his great-nephew, all he possessed. Which didn't amount to much as he had gambled just about everything away long before I came to live with him.

"Go on now, boy," Uncle Philemon told me, "and fetch me the biggest old turtle you can find."

I knew better than to put up a fuss. Armed with a long pointed pole to poke the turtle out of the mud and a basket to carry him home in, I headed for the marsh. If it had been later in the year, I would have had an easy time of it, but we'd had a long cold spell in February, worse than a normal Maryland winter, and the wily old rascals were still hibernating. I figured they'd burrowed clean through the earth to China by now. Most likely children on the other side of the world were catching turtles that by right ought to have been mine.

The wind blew across the Chesapeake Bay, straight through the tall grass, driving the cold rain before it. It pricked my face like icy needles and soaked right through my raggedy old jacket. I soon grew weary of prodding and poking the mud and finding nothing.

"Dang you, Uncle Philemon," I hollered, "and dang your everlasting rheumatism, too!"

I was sorely tempted to go home, but I didn't dare, not when my uncle had his belly primed for terrapin soup. If I walked through the door with nothing for Delia to cook, the old boy would throw a fit loud enough to scare the devil himself. Might even give me a thrashing, especially if he'd been into the brandy.

Despite his cantankerous ways, I must say I was normally right fond of my uncle. He'd done his Christian duty by me, sure enough, for he'd taken me in after Mama and Daddy died. I wasn't but four years old at the time and the most useless child you ever did see, but he agreed to be my guardian and teach me to be a carpenter. All he'd taught me so far was hammering, which you can't call a skill. I guessed it was a start, though. After all, I was only twelve. I had plenty of years to learn sawing and measuring and such.

Mostly what I did for my uncle was milk the cow, help the hired hands with the planting and harvesting, and provide Delia with things to cook for supper. Deer, squirrels, rabbits, oysters, crabs, turtles—whatever the old man wanted to eat I brung home. Without me, he'd most likely have starved to death long ago.

Other than that, and a few lessons in reading, writing, and figuring, Uncle Philemon allowed me to do pretty much as I pleased, which was often nothing but playing in the creek or climbing trees or making mischief of one kind or another. As for thrashings, all I had to do was stay out of his way when he'd been drinking. You can't ask for a much better life than that.

So I kept on poking the mud in hope of scaring up a turtle. Before long, the rain turned to a downpour so heavy I could hardly see. Truth to tell, the wetter I got, the better a thrashing seemed, mainly because it would be given inside, in front of a roaring fire. Let Uncle Philemon warm my britches—and the rest of me as well. If he wanted a turtle, he'd just have to drag his sorry old self down here and find one.

I took a path that led out of the marsh and into the woods, hoping to find shelter under the trees. If I hadn't been fussing about my uncle, I might have wondered why the crows were making such a ruckus, but I was just too mad to pay them any mind. In fact, I didn't notice a thing out of the ordinary till someone grabbed me from behind, pressed a knife against my throat, and clamped a hand over my mouth.

"Don't move or I'll kill you," a woman hissed in my ear. "Don't make a sound either. Stay right where you are, as quiet as you can be."

The hand holding the knife was brown. Since I didn't know of any Negro, slave or free, who'd dare to rob a white boy, I figured she was a runaway and desperate enough to do anything. So I did what she said. Kept my mouth shut, didn't move a finger or a toe, scarcely even breathed.

A Negro boy about seven or eight years old stepped out from behind the woman, looking every bit as desperate as his mama sounded. In one hand he held a big stick. Little as he was, I had no doubt he'd use it on me, given half a chance.

Other than the stick, the first thing I noticed about him were his eyes, which were as blue as mine. His hair was light, too, but tight curled. His clothes were torn and stained with mud, but even so, they'd once been finer than anything I'd ever owned. As far as I could tell, I'd never seen the child before, which surprised me somewhat. There weren't many slaves in this part of the county, and I knew most every one of them.

"You better do as Mama says," the boy told me, just as bold as he could be. "She'd just as soon kill you as look at you."

"Perry, for the good Lord's sake, hush." The woman tightened her grip on me. I felt her belly press against my back, as big and hard as a watermelon. "We need your help, Jesse Sherman."

It startled me to hear her speak my name, but when I tried to get a look at her face, her knife kept me from turning my head.

"If you promise to be still, I'll take my hand off your mouth," she said. "But I'm keeping the knife where it is."

I nodded, signifying I'd do as she asked. Right away, she uncovered my mouth and grabbed my arm. Like she'd promised, the hand holding the knife stayed where it was, but she allowed me to see her face.

To my surprise, I found myself staring into the eyes of

Delia's niece Lydia. I knew for a fact she belonged to the recently deceased Mr. Peregrine Baxter, who lived up the Tred Avon River from Uncle Philemon's place. Not an easy journey, especially if you was afraid to be seen on a public road. They must have gone through woods and swamps and marshes, all in the rain and the cold.

So it was no wonder Lydia looked a sight. Her hair, usually so neat and tidy, hung in her eyes, and her fine silk dress was a wreck, its ruffles torn and its skirt stained. To make matters worse, she appeared to be about as big with child as a woman can get.

Nor did she appear well. The hands holding me fast were hot, and her eyes glittered with fever. She seemed to be ailing of something besides the baby in her belly.

"What are you doing here, Lydia?" I asked. "Have you gone clear out of your mind?"

"Don't waste my time asking foolish questions," she said. "My baby's coming. I need you to fetch Miss Sally Harrison to help me." While she spoke, she kept that knife against my throat, pressing so tight I could feel its sharp edge bite into my skin.

"Lydia, you know full well Miss Sally ain't going to birth a runaway slave's baby," I said, truly believing the poor girl was off her head with swamp fever. "It's against the law to aid and abet fugitives such as yourself. Miss Sally don't want to go to jail no more than I do."

At this, Perry raised his stick as if he meant to whack me one. "You better do what my mama says."

Irked by the sassy way he spoke, I leaned close and

done my best to scare the child. "I seen Colonel Abednego Botfield just a few days ago at Mr. Baxter's funeral," I said. "He was looking meaner and uglier than ever. You know he's the Widow Baxter's uncle, don't you? I reckon she's already sent him after you and your mama."

Lydia narrowed her eyes and tightened her grip on me. There wasn't a Negro on the entire Eastern Shore who didn't know and despise Colonel Abednego Botfield's name. He was the meanest and most determined slave catcher in Talbot County—maybe in the whole state of Maryland. Once he went after a runaway, he never turned back till he caught him. Sometimes he even captured free Negroes and sold them into slavery. To hear Delia talk, the man was a hound from hell.

Truth to tell, I didn't like the colonel no better than Delia did, for he was the very card sharp who'd won just about everything Uncle Philemon owned, including my inheritance. But the law was the law, and I figured I should remind this bratty boy of the trouble he was in.

"Don't mention that devil's name again." Lydia pressed her knife against me as if she meant to slit my throat then and there. "He's caused nothing but misery since the day he was born. It should have been him who died, not Peregrine."

The tears in Lydia's eyes puzzled me. It didn't make sense for a slave to weep over a white man's death. Especially when she was running away from that very man's widow.

"Peregrine meant to free Perry and me. He promised," she went on. "But last night I heard Mrs. Henrietta tell her uncle to take us to Slattery's slave jail in Baltimore and sell us south—"

Lydia broke off with a groan. She clenched her teeth and shut her eyes, but she didn't loosen her grip on me or the knife.

"Do you know what sort of place Slattery's is?" she asked when the pain had passed.

I nodded with my head down, ashamed to meet her eyes. Slattery's was the worst slave jail in all Baltimore City. It had a reputation of pure evil. Though Uncle Philemon sometimes threatened to send Delia there, he didn't mean it and she knew it. It was just something to say when she made him mad. He always ended up apologizing to her for suggesting such a thing. After a while, she usually forgave him.

Though I wasn't overly fond of the recently widowed Mrs. Baxter, I couldn't imagine her sending a slave to Slattery's any more than I could Uncle Philemon. Didn't I see the woman every Sunday in church, wearing her best finery and looking as godly as the other ladies?

"Why would Mrs. Baxter do such a cruel thing?" I asked. "It don't make sense to send you and the child to Slattery's."

Lydia glanced at Perry and touched her belly. She didn't have to say another word. I'd heard my uncle tell of many a white man who had more than one set of blue-eyed children. Not that he knew me to be listening. It was just that he forgot himself and spoke to his friends while I sat nearby, taking everything in—including a sly puff on his cigar and a quick sip of his whiskey.

Knowing the truth didn't shock me or nothing. But it made me sad for Lydia. Thanks to Mr. Peregrine's fall from a horse, she was in a fix for sure.

Lydia squeezed my hand. "You're a good boy, Jesse. Delia's always spoken well of you. Surely I can trust you to fetch Miss Sally. That's all I'm asking you to do. Tell her and no one else where I am. Then be on your way."

Although Lydia was most likely sweet-talking me, it pleased me to hear her say I was a good boy. No one had told me that since my mama died. Most folks thought me a no-account rascal, unlikely to improve with age.

It also pleased me to know Delia spoke well of me behind my back, for she never had much good to say to my face.

Another pain hit Lydia, and she groaned again. It was clear that baby was truly on its way into the world, whether the world wanted it or not.

"Unless you know how to birth a baby," Lydia whispered, "you'd better fetch Miss Sally fast. I haven't time to argue, Jesse."

"I'll go tell her you need her," I said. "But that's all I'm doing for you. Helping a runaway is against the law. You know it as well as I do."

I spoke bold, but, truth to tell, I was scared silly.

When that baby came, there'd be blood and pain and screaming. Maybe even dying. I'd been through that when Mama died. All things considered, I figured I'd rather break the law than help at a birthing.

And, besides, there was Lydia herself, as helpless as she could be, about to have a baby in the rain with no shelter but the bare trees. Sick, too. And saddled with that bratty boy. Lord, she had more than enough woes already without me making things worse for her.

Lydia sank down on the ground, her back against a tree. "Hurry," she begged. "Tell Miss Sally I'm too far gone to risk coming to her."

I took off through the woods, running full tilt, scarcely bothering to duck the branches that whipped my face. Though I'd never been one to put much stock in prayer, I found myself calling on the Lord.

"Please let Miss Sally be home when I get there, and let her be willing to help a poor runaway slave," I prayed, breathing rough and ragged from running so hard. "Please let nobody learn what I done tonight. Don't let me get sent to jail or hanged. If you let me go home safe, I promise to be good the rest of my natural life. I'll give up smoking and drinking and lying and cussing, I promise you."

It was the most praying I'd done in or out of church, and I sincerely hoped the Lord would remember my voice and grant what I was asking.

CHAPTER 2

When I came to the road, I hunkered behind a tree and listened and looked as hard as I could, fearful Colonel Abednego Botfield might be nearby, searching for Lydia and the boy. I wouldn't have wanted to run into him tonight, not knowing what I knew. Praise be, I heard nothing but the drip-drop of rain and the wind sighing in the branches, and I saw nothing but dark fields and woods. Not far away, a light shone in Miss Sally's window. It seemed the Lord had granted at least one of my prayers, for no one goes off and leaves a lamp burning in an empty house.

Taking one long last look and listen, I darted across the road to Miss Sally's place and knocked softly.

The old woman opened the door almost at once and peered out at me. She was close to Uncle Philemon in years, a bony little bird of a thing, all sharp angles and as full of sass as a blue jay. Nobody in these parts dared vex her. Whenever someone was needed to birth a baby or tend the sick and dying, folks sent for Miss Sally Harrison. If she couldn't help, nobody could.

"Why, Jesse," Miss Sally said, "what brings you here? Is Philemon took bad with his belly again?"

"No, ma'am, it ain't my uncle that's ailing. It's something altogether worse." I hesitated and took a deep breath. "It's the Baxters' house slave, Lydia—" I began, but the look on Miss Sally's face stopped me dead.

"She's run away, ain't she? Soon as I heard of Peregrine's death, I feared she'd do something foolish."

I stared at the old woman in wonderment. Lord, she beat all for knowing everything and everybody. "Yes, ma'am," I said, "that's just what Lydia done. But that's not why I've come. She's hiding in the woods, about to birth a baby. I know she's a slave, but she's in a terrible bad way and she asked for you special. She'll die if she don't get help. I swear she will."

Miss Sally heaved a deep sigh. "Don't you fret, Jesse. That poor young woman won't die in the woods if I can help it." Taking time to blow out her lamp, the old woman grabbed a lantern and followed me across the road and into the woods. For an old lady, she kept up with me pretty good, hopping over dead branches like a sparrow in the spring.

"Why didn't you bring Lydia to the house?" Miss Sally asked.

"She's too far gone to walk," I said. "And she's a runaway. What if someone seen her coming to your door?" I stopped and looked at the old woman. "You won't tell the colonel, will you?"

Miss Sally studied my face in the lantern light. "Jesse, I freed my slaves years ago, as all decent folk should. Believe me, the very last thing I'd do is report a runaway."

At that moment, we heard Lydia cry out from the darkness. Miss Sally picked up her feet fast and hastened toward the sound, leaving me to chase after her as best I could.

Lydia sat where I'd left her, leaning against the tree. In the lantern light, she looked even more sick and feverish than before. Perry crouched beside her, his face full of fear and worry.

Miss Sally dropped to her knees beside Lydia. "How close are the pains, my dear?"

"Just a few minutes apart, maybe less." Lydia moaned as another wave took a hold of her body.

The old woman sucked in her breath and thrust the lantern at me. "Hold this, Jesse."

"But, Miss Sally," I said. "I done my part by bringing you here. I got to go home now. My uncle—"

Miss Sally fixed me with her sharp eyes. "You ain't going nowhere, Jesse Sherman. I can't do this all by myself."

I could see the old lady's mind was made up. No amount of arguing would get me free. Though my knees were weak and my belly was queasy, I done as she asked and held the lantern. Its light flickered on the ground and the bushes, giving everything the look of a stage lit by candles. But what was about to happen was no play. And I had no wish to see it.

Perry stood back, too. I reckoned he was scared, and I couldn't blame him. My mama had died birthing a baby. A little sister it would have been, but she'd died, too. Never opened her eyes to this world. From the womb to the tomb, I'd heard someone say, with no earthly life in between.

Then, just a few months later, my dear daddy died of pneumonia, and I found myself an orphan with nowhere to go but Uncle Philemon's tumbledown plantation house. Now it seemed Perry might soon be in the same plight. But it would be worse for him. If something happened to his mama, he wouldn't have no Uncle Philemon to take him, no shelter, no nothing. It didn't bear thinking about.

When Lydia started screaming, Miss Sally done her best to calm her with talk of how it would be better soon, but the old woman kept praying and calling on God. That struck me as a bad sign. It seemed to me the Lord was often listening to someone else's prayers when you needed Him most.

"Hold that lantern steady, Jesse!" Miss Sally shouted. "How do you expect me to see what I'm doing?"

"I didn't mean to swing it," I said. "I just never seen, I mean I, I . . ."

Miss Sally gave me such a look I hushed and did my best to keep my hands from shaking. But it was true.

Before now, I'd only had a dim notion of the pain a woman suffered bringing a baby into the world. When Mama died, I'd been on the back porch with my daddy. I hadn't been right there in the room with her, seeing as well as hearing.

The next time Lydia screamed, Perry commenced to cry. Shoving me out of the way, he ran to his mother's side and flung himself on her. "Mama, Mama," he wept.

Lydia pushed him away and Miss Sally grabbed him. "Set the lantern on the ground, Jesse, and take this child somewhere."

"No, no," Perry wailed. "I want to stay with Mama."

I knew how he felt, but, sorry as I was for him, I dragged him off into the woods. I had to fight him every step of the way. If he'd been any bigger, I doubt I could have kept him from going back to his mother.

At the edge of the marsh, Perry turned to me, sagging like the fight had gone clear out of him. "Mama won't die, will she?"

The tall grass blew in the wind, making the saddest sound I ever heard. "Miss Sally will do her best to save your mama," I said, "but . . ."

"But what?"

I looked at Perry then. Tears ran down his cheeks, and he was shivering. Never had I seen a child so miserable. Instead of telling him about my own mama, I choked the words off with a shrug. "I don't know," I said, feeling every bit as bad as he did.

Perry picked up a stone and threw it into the marsh.

He picked up another and threw it even farther. I joined in. Stone after stone splashed into the water. We didn't say a word—just threw those stones as if somebody was paying us to do it.

At long last Miss Sally called us. Perry hurled one more stone and followed me back to the tree. In the lantern's light, I saw Lydia lying on the cold ground, holding a tiny baby. Miss Sally knelt beside her. All around them were the dark woods. Rain dripped and gurgled and splashed down through the trees. There was no other sound. It reminded me of the Christmas pageant at church, where people pose as the Virgin Mary and the shepherds and angels and never move nor speak. Only there was just Mary and the baby in this scene.

Before I could stop him, Perry ran to Lydia. He didn't so much as look at the baby. "Mama, Mama," he cried, throwing himself down beside her.

I grabbed Miss Sally's hand. "The baby," I whispered. "Is it . . . Is it . . ." Somehow I couldn't bring myself to say what I feared.

The old woman sighed and put her arm around me. "Stillborn," she whispered. "There was nothing I could do, nothing at all. The dear little girl's safe with our Lord now."

Sad as the news was, it didn't surprise me none. In this world, more babies died than lived. "How about Lydia?"

"Worn out," Miss Sally said slowly, "and sick with

fever. Worse yet, she's bleeding so bad I'm afraid to move her."

"Don't let her die," I begged. "Oh, please, Miss Sally. I can't bear no more people dying."

"It's up to the good Lord now," Miss Sally said. "I've done all I can, Jesse."

Her words didn't comfort me. As far as I could tell, the sight of people dying didn't bother the Lord nearly as much as it bothered me. Maybe He was used to it. After all, folks had been dying in one way or another since Adam and Eve ate that fool apple and brought sin and death into the world.

Perry huddled beside his mother, talking low and stroking her face, but I squatted under a tree and watched Miss Sally pace back and forth, praying to Jesus to spare Lydia.

Suddenly Lydia reached up and grabbed Miss Sally's skirt, pulled her close, and whispered to her. Miss Sally straightened up and beckoned to me. "Jesse, come here. Lydia wants to ask you something."

I crouched down beside Lydia, keeping my eyes away from that baby but seeing it anyway, pale and waxy and stiller than stone. Its eyes were closed, but I felt it was watching me somehow, waiting to see what I'd do and hear what I'd say.

Lydia grasped my hand. Her skin was so hot it burned my flesh, but I didn't pull away. I let her draw me closer till I was looking straight into her eyes. "I was bound for Baltimore City," she whispered, "to see Peregrine's sister,

Miss Polly Baxter." She paused a moment to catch her breath, but her grip on me didn't loosen. "If something happens to me, can I count on you to take Perry to her?"

"You told me to fetch Miss Sally and then I could go my way," I objected. "Surely you can't expect me to take a runaway slave child all the way to Baltimore. Why, that's just crazy. I—"

Perry shoved me aside and crouched close to his mama. "I won't go without you, Mama. Not with that boy, not with anyone! I'm staying right here with you, even if, even if . . ." His voice trailed away and his eyes filled with tears.

I knew his meaning. If Lydia died, he'd lie down and die, too. I'd tried that myself the night Mama died. But here I was, skinny and small for my age but still alive. And likely to stay that way if I kept close to home. Traipsing off to Baltimore like some cussed abolitionist was bound to shorten my life.

"Please, Perry," Lydia whispered. "Polly is my dear friend, as close to me as a sister. She'll love you just as she loved Peregrine. You're so like your father."

"What if she doesn't want me?" he cried. "She doesn't know about me. You never told her—"

"Hush." Lydia pulled at a chain around her neck till it broke. Pressing a silver locket into Perry's hands, she said, "Give Polly this."

Perry opened the little heart. Inside were two paintings no bigger than my thumbnail. One was of Mr. Peregrine Baxter and the other was of Lydia.

"You see?" Lydia whispered. "When you show Polly that, she'll know her brother loved us."

Lydia turned to me. "Jesse, give me your solemn word you'll take Perry to Miss Polly Baxter, number 115 West Monument Street."

"But Lydia—" I began.

"Please help my son," Lydia said. "If you refuse, what will become of him?"

Well, the answer to that was simple enough. The child would no doubt fall into the colonel's hands and end up at Slattery's, where he'd most likely die of disease. How could I bear such a thing on my conscience? Though it meant breaking the law, I heard myself promise to take Perry to Baltimore City, a place I'd never been and knew nothing about except it was a half day's journey up the Bay and full of corruption of every sort. At least that's what Uncle Philemon said. He went there once, lost a great sum of money in a card game, and came home with bilious complaints.

Lydia smiled. "I knew you were a good boy, Jesse." Taking Perry's hand, she joined it with mine. "I trust you both to help each other," she murmured. "And to become friends."

Perry and I looked at each other but said nothing. It was clear he didn't wish to be friends with me any more than I wished to be friends with him.

Lydia let our hands go and lay back, her face peaceful. "Come closer, Perry. Keep me warm. I'm so cold, so weary."

Miss Sally touched my shoulder. "Let Lydia rest now, Jesse. But stay nearby in case I need you."

I huddled under a tree all by myself and fretted about the promise I'd just made. It seemed I'd gotten myself into a terrible fix. All that would save me was Lydia. If she lived, she'd take Perry to Miss Polly Baxter herself, and I'd be free to stay on the shore, hunting turtles and such for my uncle as if none of this had happened.

But if she died, I'd be forced to keep my word. A promise given to the dead is a sacred thing. Break it, and I'd never have a moment's peace. Lydia would haunt me forever, following me wherever I went.

A long time passed. The rain stopped once and started up again. The wind rose and fell. Down in the marsh, spring peepers made a glad noise, which seemed out of keeping with things. I wished they'd hush.

At last Miss Sally came to me, her face full of sorrow, and told me Lydia was dead. My heart filled with sadness for her and Perry and the poor little baby that never took a breath of air. While Miss Sally rocked Perry in her arms, trying to hush his sobs, I shed a few tears of my own for Lydia and Mama both.

After a while, Miss Sally came to me again and whispered, "Go back to my house, Jesse, and fetch two shovels from the shed. And bring the quilt from my bed to wrap her in. The white one with the wedding ring pattern. It's my very best."

. I stared at Miss Sally, shocked. "Surely we ain't burying Lydia out here in the woods?"

"What else can we do, Jesse? We've got to hide her from the colonel. He'll be back to my house, like as not, nosing around, doing his best to put me in the jail house."

"But you're the best midwife in these parts and the best healer, too. Why would the colonel want to lock you up?"

Miss Sally looked me hard in the eye. "Nobody's proved it yet, but folks suspicion I've been helping fugitives go north for some years now. You know how slave owners feel about aiding and abetting."

I was speechless. All this time I'd thought Miss Sally was just an old Methodist lady who birthed babies and treated the ill and prayed hard for the dying. I'd never dreamed she was helping runaways.

"Go on now, Jesse," Miss Sally begged, "and, for the Lord's sake, keep your mouth shut when you go home. If Philemon gets wind of this, you know what will happen."

She meant the old man couldn't keep a thing to himself, especially after he'd had a few whiskies at the tavern.

"I won't say nothing," I promised. And how could I? I'd broken the law myself tonight, starting when I went for Miss Sally instead of the sheriff. Worse yet, I was likely to continue my life of crime till I was rid of Perry.

So I done what she asked and set out for her house with a heart full of misgivings.

CHAPTER 3

Just as I neared Miss Sally's place, a horseman came riding toward me, going slow, as if he was looking for something. Or someone. I tried to hide behind a tree, but Colonel Abednego Botfield was as sharp-eyed as an owl in pursuit of a mouse.

"Hey there, Jesse," he called softly. "What keeps you out so late on a rainy night? You got a sweetheart already?"

"I been hunting turtles, sir." Dry mouthed with fright, I scuttled past him as fast as a crab heading for deep water. "Missed my way in the marsh. Now I got to hurry. Uncle Philemon's bound to be looking for me."

"Slow down a second and let me ask you a question." Colonel Botfield blocked my way with his horse, a big bay with eyes as mean as his owner's.

I figured the bay would just as soon step on me as not, so I came to a stop and peered up at Colonel

Botfield. I kept a good distance between us in case he made a grab for me. His slouch hat dipped low over his face, shadowing every feature except his mustache, so it was hard to tell what he aimed to do.

"I'm looking for the wench that ran off from the Widow Baxter," he said. "Name of Lydia. Light-complected, big bellied with child, had a boy with her. Pretty but insolent in her manner. You seen her? My niece wants her back real bad."

"No, sir," I whispered. "I ain't met a soul all day."

Colonel Botfield spat through his teeth into the mud at my feet. "You sure about that, Jesse? You wouldn't lie to me, would you, boy?"

"Hiding a runaway slave's against the law, sir."

Colonel Botfield pulled out a cigar. The flare from his match lit a face I'd have preferred not to see. "There's a reward for the wench and the boy both. Valuable property, you know. With or without your help, I reckon I'll track her down."

He studied my face, his eyes narrowed to slits. "No runaways escape Abednego Botfield," he said. "Not when he sets his mind on catching 'em."

I stood there in the road, my knees knocking, almost too scared to breathe. Cold rain trickled down the back of my neck. The wind blew through my damp jacket and trousers. I'd have given anything to be home safe in bed.

Keeping his eyes on me, Colonel Botfield nudged the horse. "Step on, sir." The big bay obeyed at once.

No doubt he'd known the feel of his owner's whip many a time.

"You be sure and tell me if you see the woman," Colonel Botfield called back. "If I'm feeling generous, I might give you a nickel for the information—if it leads to her capture, that is."

He turned then and rode off into the rain. I wanted to holler after him he'd never find Lydia. Never, never, never. She was far beyond his reach or anyone else's. But I kept my mouth shut and let him go, glad to see his back.

When I was sure the man was really and truly gone, I slipped through Miss Sally's garden, found the shovels in her shed, grabbed the quilt off her bed, and sneaked back into the woods.

Perry and Miss Sally were sheltered under the tree where I'd left them. Despite everything, the poor boy had fallen fast asleep, his head on his mother's breast, his arms holding her tight.

"Where have you been, Jesse?" Miss Sally asked. "This child should be in a warm, dry bed. I fear he's sickening from fever himself."

"I ran smack into Colonel Abednego Botfield," I answered. "He held me up with a heap of questions about Lydia and Perry. He wants them real bad. There's a big reward and he aims to collect it."

Miss Sally clenched her fists. "May heaven protect us from that godless villain," she prayed. Then, taking one shovel, she led me away from Perry and Lydia.

"While you were gone, I found a good place under that pine over there," she told me. "The ground seems easy to dig. And it's out of sight of the path."

After that, we didn't say much. Just dug and dug, making the hole long and narrow, deeper and deeper. Dirt turned to mud, slipping and sliding back into the hole. Roots snagged our shovels, but we kept at it. It wouldn't do for Lydia to be found by a fox or a wild pig. Or Colonel Abednego Botfield's dogs. We wanted her and that poor little baby to sleep undisturbed.

Behind us we heard Perry crying. It was the saddest, loneliest sound I'd ever heard. Worse than wind blowing through bare trees, worse than an owl hooting deep in the woods on a rainy night, worse than a hound howling at the moon.

"I'd best go to him," Miss Sally said. "I need to prepare Lydia's body for burial, too."

I leaned on my shovel and watched her walk off through the trees. She was a right spry old lady. Too bad Uncle Philemon didn't have her grit. Why, if he'd tried to help me shovel, I'd have ended up burying him as well as Lydia.

When I judged the grave to be deep enough, I went to tell Miss Sally. While I'd been digging, she'd wrapped Lydia and the baby in the quilt. It came to me the old woman might have begun that quilt when she was a girl, still hoping to marry. Back in those long-ago days, she'd never have guessed what use she'd finally put it to. It fair gave me the shivers to think such thoughts.

Miss Sally put her hand on Perry's shoulder. "It's time to say good-bye to your mother," she said softly. "I know it's hard, but you must be brave, Perry. It's what your mama would want of you."

Perry jerked away from her. "You're not burying my mama in these woods!" he declared. "I won't let you!"

Miss Sally took his arm again. "Perry, darling, it's the only way to keep her from being found."

He shook his head, his eyes running over with misery. "It's raining and the ground's muddy and cold," he sobbed. "She'll be all alone. She'll think nobody loves her."

"Please, Perry," Miss Sally begged. "Your mama wants you to be safe. She don't want you taking sick here in the woods."

It took a powerful heap of coaxing, but at last Perry allowed Miss Sally and me to carry Lydia's body to the grave we'd dug. He walked along beside us, keeping one hand on his mama.

The hole was already filling with water, seeping up from the marshy ground. I didn't want to put Lydia and her baby down there any more than Perry did.

"How are we going to do it?" I asked Miss Sally. "At church they lower the coffin on ropes, but we ain't got a coffin or a rope."

Miss Sally sighed and picked up one end of the bundle. With a heavy heart, I took the other end. There just wasn't no proper way to do what had to be done. Slowly we eased our burden over the edge and let it fall with a terrible splash into the muddy water at the bottom.

Perry let out a howl of pure misery that gave me goosebumps. If Miss Sally hadn't stopped him, I swear he'd have jumped in after his mother. While they struggled, I stared into the grave, half hoping Lydia would shake the quilt off, sit up, and ask what she was doing down there. But the bundle lay where it had fallen, as still as if it contained nothing but a log.

When I reached for the shovel, Miss Sally laid a hand on my arm. "We have to say some prayers first," she said. "It's not proper to send her off without the Lord's blessing on her soul."

Somehow Miss Sally quieted Perry. Taking his hand and mine, she spoke the proper words from the Prayer Book. I'd heard them at burials so often I knew them by heart, too. "I am the resurrection and the life, saith the Lord: he that believeth in me, though he were dead, yet shall he live: and whosoever liveth and believeth in me, shall never die."

The wind blew through the treetops, and the rain fell softly, more like a fine mist now, but still cold, still wet. I knew Miss Sally meant to comfort Perry with her prayers, but the boy kept sobbing as if his heart was broke to pieces.

"For as much as it hath pleased Almighty God of His great mercy to take unto Himself the soul of our dear sister here departed," Miss Sally prayed on, "we therefore commit her body to the ground; earth to earth, ashes to ashes, dust to dust; in sure and certain hope of the Resurrection to eternal life."

Miss Sally picked up a handful of earth and dropped it into the grave. Recalling all the burials I'd attended, I dropped another handful. It was the right and proper thing to do, but I hated the sound and I hoped the dead couldn't hear it.

Perry dropped nothing into the grave. He stood beside Miss Sally, clasping one of her hands and crying for his mama.

"May your soul and your baby's soul rest in peace through the mercy of God," Miss Sally whispered to Lydia.

"Amen," I ended.

We stood there a while, listening to the wind and thinking our own thoughts, mainly wishing things had turned out different. Neither Miss Sally nor me wanted to pick up those shovels and fill that grave.

At last Miss Sally took me aside and whispered, "I hate to leave you here, Jesse, but I ought to take Perry home. He don't need to see his mama buried under all that dirt."

She was right. Even though it meant leaving me alone in the woods with the dead, it was best to spare Perry the sight of what had to be done.

"Come by the house when you're finished," she said. "We got plans to make."

It took some persuasion to get Perry to depart. Poor boy, he didn't want to leave his mama. Finally Miss Sally all but dragged him away.

Once they were gone, I picked up a shovel and

began my sad task. When I was done filling the grave, I packed the dirt down and covered the fresh soil with dead leaves and fallen branches to make it look like nobody had disturbed the ground. Before I left, I promised Lydia I'd come back when it was safe and put up a proper marker.

"I'll carve your name on it," I told her, "and the date you departed this world, but for now I got to keep you hidden."

It may sound peculiar, but I had a feeling Lydia was close by, watching me, waiting for me to say more. Swallowing hard, I spoke the words I knew she wanted to hear. "Don't you worry none about Perry. I'll get him safe to Baltimore, I swear I will."

There was no backing out now. No matter how I dreaded taking that boy anywhere, I had to keep my promise to Lydia. As much as I admired her, I knew she'd make a fearsome ghost. Especially if she thought I'd let anything bad happen to Perry.

Fearful of seeing or hearing I don't know what, I ran all the way to Miss Sally's house. When I got there, she heard me putting the shovels in the shed and opened her back door. "You done well tonight, Jesse."

I shrugged. Digging a hole wasn't nothing to brag on. "I just wish she hadn't died."

Miss Sally smiled and patted my head like she was fond of me, which came as a surprise. "Do you think you can get Perry to Miss Polly Baxter in Baltimore City?"

"I promised his mama I would."

"You ever been there?"

"No, ma'am. I ain't never been anywhere but here."

Miss Sally sighed. "I'd go myself, but Colonel Botfield's got his eye on me for sure. He passed the house twice while you were filling in the grave. Once he paused at the gate like he was considering coming to the door, but he went on, thank the good Lord. It's lucky Perry's sleeping sound. If he'd cried out, the colonel would have been on him like a hawk."

I looked behind me, fearing the old devil might be coming along the road as we spoke, but I saw nothing. Didn't hear hoofbeats either, just the everlasting drizzle of the rain and the soft murmur of the wind, bringing the salt smell of the bay to my nose.

"My brother William's taking a boatload of fish to Baltimore before dawn Friday. He'll be glad to take you two along with him. Most likely I can keep Perry safe till then." Miss Sally patted my head. "You go along home and get some sleep, Jesse. You look plain tuckered out."

It wasn't till I came in sight of my uncle's house that I remembered the turtle. I'd left the basket and the pole down in the woods, but I wasn't going back for them. Not now. Nor was I going to worry about a thrashing. No doubt my uncle was sound asleep, snoring up a storm, with no thought of me. Or that dang turtle either.

I crept to the back door and let myself in as quietly

as a burglar. Not a sound, not a light. Five or six of my uncle's hounds slept in front of the kitchen fire, snuffling and snorting, twitching like they were dreaming of rabbits and foxes.

With two hounds following me, I tiptoed to the larder and stuffed myself on cold ham, biscuits, and cheese. Didn't forget to share some with the dogs either. Then up to bed I went, grateful to peel off my wet clothes and slide beneath the covers, warm and dry and safe for now.

But all too soon I'd be running off to Baltimore City with a slave child, going against everything I'd been taught. Perry belonged to the Widow Henrietta Baxter. That was the pure and simple truth. If I found the widow's horse running loose along the road, would I let it go on its way and say nothing? Of course not. Even if the widow treated the poor horse badly, I was bound by law to take it to her. It was the same with slaves. If you caught a runaway, you were bound by law to help his owners get him back. What folks did with their possessions had nothing whatsoever to do with the legality of things.

Up till now I hadn't given the matter any thought. In fact, I'd often daydreamed about capturing a runaway slave and turning him in for a reward. Of course, the slave of my fancies was always a big strong man with an evil reputation, one who'd cut his owner's throat and burned down the plantation house and was terrorizing the countryside. Catching a slave like that would be an act of heroism.

Somehow turning a little orphan boy over to the sheriff didn't measure up to the daring deed I'd imagined.

Then something else occurred to me. What if I got caught helping Perry? Would a bunch of men come for me in the night and hang me, like they done old Jacob Withers when he helped ten slaves cross the border into Delaware? Or would they be more likely to forgive a twelve-year-old boy?

Tormented by these thoughts and more, I burrowed under the covers. If only Uncle Philemon hadn't gotten that craving for turtle soup. If only I hadn't gone into the woods for shelter. If only Lydia had grabbed hold of some other boy.

But no matter how hard you wish things to be different, you can't change anything once it's happened. I was bound to go to Baltimore City with Perry. Whether I wanted to or not. It was my fate, I reckoned, and how it would all play out I had no idea.

CHAPTER 4

The next morning, I delayed going downstairs for as long as I dared, but by ten my empty belly drove me to the kitchen. Delia looked up from the dough she was kneading, her dark hands slapping it this way and that, punching it hard.

"Where in tarnation have you been?" she asked. "Your uncle had to go up to bed last night without that terrapin soup he was craving. Put him in a mighty foul humor, too. Good thing you wasn't here. He'd have whupped you good."

I picked up a piece of raw dough and rolled it in my hands like clay until it was as long and skinny as a snake. I longed to tell Delia the truth. As kin to Lydia, she ought to know what had happened. But I'd promised Lydia not to say a word to anyone—and that included her aunt. So, without raising my eyes from the dough, I claimed I'd been doing just what

I'd been told—hunting turtles for hours in the marsh.

"I told your uncle April is too early for turtles," Delia said with some satisfaction. "You won't find them critters for another two, three weeks at least. Not unless you light a fire and make them think it's warm, and how you going to do that in the pouring-down rain?"

She clucked her tongue and turned the dough, slapping it silly. "Pure foolishness sending you on such an errand. It's a wonder you ain't half dead of fever."

"Where's Uncle Philemon now?" I asked, my mouth full of biscuit and ham.

"Oh, Colonel Abednego Botfield come by the house this morning. He and Mr. Philemon went into town together, all excited. Something to do with that fort down in South Carolina."

I'd heard enough talk to know what Delia meant. "Did the Confederates fire on Fort Sumter?"

Delia shrugged her broad shoulders. "I believe so."

My heart beat a little faster. "Are we going to war?"

"The colonel didn't share no news with me." Delia started humming to herself, a sure sign she'd told me all she planned to. Turning her back, she started raking up the fire.

But I couldn't let matters rest. "Do you favor the North or the South, Delia?"

She gave me a long look. "If you had the sense you were born with, you'd go on down to the marsh and find your silly self a turtle before your uncle comes home."

The marsh was the last place on earth I wanted to

go, but I took her advice and headed out the door. Wouldn't do no good to hang around the kitchen plying her with questions. She wasn't about to say anything more about the war.

Didn't have to, really. No doubt she was for the North and that rascal Mr. Lincoln. If the Yankees won, she wouldn't have to wait for Uncle Philemon to die to be free.

Keeping an eye out for the colonel, I went down to the woods. My pole and basket lay where I'd dropped them the day before. Though I didn't dare linger, I took a quick look at Lydia's grave. I didn't think anyone would notice it, even in daylight.

For the rest of the morning, I poked around in the marsh, hunting turtles with my pole. The rain had stopped, but the sky and the water were the same dull gray and the wind was cold. Seemed spring would be late this year.

Around noon, I got lucky and caught me a turtle dumb enough to have come out of the mud a little too early. It wasn't a big one, but I figured it would do.

As I headed home, I saw Colonel Abednego Botfield riding toward me on the narrow path. It seemed there was no avoiding the man.

"Well, well, Jesse, we meet again." The old devil touched the brim of his slouch hat. I'd heard folks say he was once a fine-looking man, but his face showed the battering of time and the life he'd led. A scar here, a scar there, teeth as crooked as gravestones, eyes veined, the skin under them hanging in loose folds. He was smoking a cigar, and the reek of it was worse than the smell of marsh mud.

"Surely you ain't hunting turtles again today," he said in that low, drawly voice of his that made my skin crawl.

I held the basket up to show him what was inside. "Yes, sir. Caught one, too."

The colonel didn't bother to look at the turtle. "You seen that woman today? The one I asked you about last night?"

"No, sir." I shifted my weight from one foot to the other and studied my turtle like he was the most fascinating critter ever seen, though he weren't doing a thing but lying there all sealed up in his shell.

Colonel Botfield slapped the reins against the horse's neck, and nudged him toward me. The big bay rolled his eyes and stepped this way and that, swishing his tail.

"Easy, sir, easy," the colonel whispered. "It's just a no-'count scalawag boy. We could eat him for supper if we had a mind to."

The horse was so close I could feel the heat of his body and smell the sweet odor of his sweat. To keep from being trampled, I stepped off the path into mud up to my ankles. My heart was beating fast and loud, and I hoped to heaven the colonel couldn't hear it. It wouldn't do for him to know I was scared of him. Might make him even more suspicious than he already was.

Colonel Botfield grinned as if he found my predicament humorous. "I'll ask you once more," he said. "Are you positive you ain't seen Lydia and her boy? Tell me the truth now, for I'm certain she's hiding somewhere nearby."

"I told you last night I hadn't seen her, and I'm telling you the same today. I ain't no abolitionist." I scowled at him. "Now leave me be. I got to take this here turtle home to Uncle Philemon."

"Don't get sassy with me, Jesse Sherman." Before I realized what he was doing, Colonel Botfield leaned down and grabbed the front of my shirt, lifting me right out of the mud. The basket tipped and the turtle I'd worked so hard to catch fell out.

"Look what you done!" I shouted.

"Aw, now, don't cry, little girl. I'm just funning with you." Colonel Botfield let go then, giving me a push as he did so. I landed flat on my back in the mud. By the time I scrambled to my feet, the turtle had sunk out of sight in the marsh.

"I hope your uncle thrashes you good for coming home empty-handed again," the colonel said. "He was in a right rare old mood when I left him at the tavern."

Without another word, he thumped his heels against the horse's sides and rode off.

I cussed as hard as I could at the man's back, glad for the lessons I'd learned in such matters from my uncle, the poet of profanity. Then I buckled down and hunted that dang turtle for almost hour. They're slow-moving critters, and I hoped to get lucky and catch him before he burrowed too deep in the marsh. Which I finally did. Soon as I had him back in the basket, none the worse for his adventure, I lit out for home.

Delia seemed pleased to see my catch. "I'll get to work on that rascal right now," she said. "Ought to have him ready for supper tonight."

Not long after, Uncle Philemon came home, red in the face and smelling of the tavern. "Jesse," he shouted. "The war has commenced. The Confederates fired on Fort Sumter yesterday, and that dastard Mr. Lincoln is bound to call up the army against South Carolina."

Uncle Philemon paused to pour himself a glass of brandy. "A toast to the war," he cried, "and all the valiant men who are willing to fight for their rights."

I doubted he himself planned to be among that glorious number, but I kept my opinions to myself. It made no sense to rile him. We weren't clear on the turtle matter yet.

By the time Delia served the turtle soup, Uncle Philemon had just about brought the war to a conclusion. He saw victory for the South, of course, and the impeachment or maybe even the hanging of that villainous scoundrel in the White House.

When he finally ran out of things to say about the war and Mr. Abraham Lincoln, he turned to me. "By the way, Jesse, Abednego told me he saw you out in the rain last night, close by Miss Sally Harrison's place. Said you claimed to have been hunting turtles."

"Yes, sir, I was," I managed to say. "You sent me down to the marsh to find one, remember?"

"I don't recollect your bringing no turtle home last night."

I pointed at the tureen in front of him. "I had bad luck yesterday so I went out again today."

Uncle Philemon studied my face. His little spectacles reflected the candlelight. "Abednego told me you acted a trifle peculiar," he went on, "like you had something to hide."

"No, sir," I said. "It was cold and dark, and I was soaked through. I just wanted to go home, that's all—not stand in the rain jawing with him."

Uncle Philemon kept on staring at me, his eyes sharp despite the dim light. "Abednego's hunting a slave woman that run off from his niece's plantation. Young and pretty. Got a child with her—a boy, I believe he said. And one in her belly, too."

Delia was standing nearby, waiting to serve more soup. She gasped and almost dropped the ladle. "Mr. Philemon, are you speaking of Mrs. Baxter's house girl, Lydia?"

Uncle Philemon turned his head, obviously surprised to hear Delia speak up like that. "Why, what's it to you if I am?"

"Have you forgot Lydia's my niece?" Delia came closer to the table. "I knew Mr. Peregrine Baxter had died, but I haven't heard anything about Lydia running away."

"Well, it seems that's just what she done—run off a few days back. The Widow Baxter's got her uncle searching the marsh for her. Figures she's hiding down there. She's offering a big reward, wants her back real bad."

Delia drew in her breath. "Not him," she whispered. "Why, you know as well as I do that he's—"

Uncle Philemon gave Delia a look that silenced her. "Stories," he said. "Nothing but slaves' gossip. Even if it's true, Lydia don't mean nothing to him, her or the boy either. All Abednego wants is the reward."

Pausing to slurp up a spoonful of soup, he turned back to me. "The Widow Baxter's offering one hundred dollars to get Lydia and the boy back. That's a considerable amount."

I fidgeted with a crust of Delia's fresh baked bread. "Colonel Botfield might as well give up on her," I said, acting as if I cared nothing for Lydia's fate. "Most likely she drowned in the marsh."

"Oh, sweet Lord, don't let that be true," Delia prayed. "Lydia's young, just starting this life. She can't be dead."

I felt mighty bad for Delia, but there was no telling what Uncle Philemon would say if he got wind of what I knew and what I was about to do. So I kept eating, though by now I'd lost my appetite and had to choke my food down.

"I'll tell you true," Uncle Philemon said to Delia, "harsh as it sounds, the poor gal's better off dead. I hear

Peregrine's widow gave Abednego Botfield orders to take her and the boy to Slattery's slave jail and sell them south. Don't know what your niece done to offend the widow, but her big belly just might have some bearing on it."

Delia hid her face in her hands. "I reckon I know who's responsible for that," she muttered through her fingers.

"I hear he fathered the boy, too," Uncle Philemon said. "Now the fellow's dead. Killed falling off his horse. Oh, it's terrible sad how fast misfortune comes to us all."

Delia glanced at me and frowned as if she'd forgotten I was sitting there, listening to every word. "You look poorly, Jesse. Why don't you go on up to bed and get yourself some rest?"

Uncle Philemon nodded. "Yes, run along, boy. You shouldn't have been out in all that wind and rain. Not good for a child. Get pneumonia that way."

Delia gave him one of her sharp looks. "My, my, Mr. Philemon, you sure do change your tune, don't you?"

Uncle Philemon paused with a spoonful of soup halfway to his mouth. "What the devil do you mean, Delia?"

"Wasn't it you who sent Jesse down to the marsh, claiming bad weather was no threat to a boy his age?"

Uncle Philemon's face flushed. "I said no such thing, Delia. And don't you go arguefying with me, or I'll send you off to Slattery's to join your niece."

"Yes, sir, Mr. Philemon." Delia picked up the soup tureen and headed for the kitchen, more mad than scared.

"Now, now, Delia, don't go off in a huff," Uncle Philemon called after her, shouting to be heard above the clatter of dishes. "You know I didn't mean it. I ain't sending you nowheres."

Delia poked her head into the dining room. "Just make sure that boy goes to bed. I don't want him getting sick on account of your old turtle."

"You heard Delia," Uncle Philemon said. "Go on upstairs, Jesse."

When he spoke, I was already halfway up the steps and glad to go. I couldn't bear to hear one more word about Colonel Abednego Botfield, the Widow Baxter, Lydia, or anyone else, living or dead, slave or free. I just wanted to go to sleep and forget the mess I'd gotten myself into.

CHAPTER 5

The next day was Sunday, which meant church. Reverend Greenberry went through his prayers and familiar routines, but after he read the Gospel, he gripped the sides of the lectern and gazed out at us with a worried look.

"I'm going to base my sermon today on a reading that comes up later in the church year," he said. "The times being what they are, my conscience demands I speak out. And I can find no better words than those of the prophet Ezekiel, chapter two, verses one through seven."

Clearing his throat, Reverend Greenberry began to read from the Bible in his shrill Yankee voice: "Son of man, I send you to the children of Israel, to a rebellious nation that hath rebelled against me. . . . they are impudent children and stiffhearted. . . . be not afraid of them . . . though briers and thorns be with thee, and thou dost dwell among scorpions: be not afraid of their words, nor be dismayed at their looks, though they be a rebellious house. . . . speak my words unto them, whether they will hear, or whether they will forbear: for they are most rebellious."

It didn't take anyone long to figure out where Reverend Greenberry was heading with this reading. People began to shift and stir. They whispered among themselves. The second time the reverend said "rebellious," Uncle Philemon began thumping his cane on the floor. Others cleared their throats and twitched and coughed.

Reverend Greenberry peered at us. "A rebellious house," he repeated as if we hadn't already heard. "Any state that leaves this union blessed by God Almighty is indeed a rebellious house and will have no favor in the eyes of the Lord."

Uncle Philemon thumped his cane even harder. Several other gentlemen joined him. A familiar voice in the back of the church drawled, "Yankee fool." I looked around and saw the Widow Baxter, dressed in black, her face hidden by a veil. Her uncle, Colonel Abednego Botfield, slouched beside her, eyeing the reverend with scorn.

"The Lord is asking us to speak out, just as He asked Ezekiel." Reverend Greenberry spoke louder and smote the Bible with his fist. "The Lord wants us to speak the truth, to stand up for justice and freedom for all. If Mr. Abraham Lincoln calls upon us to take a stand against the rebels, we must go where he bids us and do what he asks!

Above all, this state must not join the house of rebellion!"

Unfortunately for Reverend Greenberry, there were few who agreed with him. It was shocking to hear them shout and call out against him and pound the floor. Never had I seen such carrying on in church. Truth to tell, it scared me.

"Go preach to the Methodists," Uncle Philemon bellowed. "You'll find fertile ground among them abolitionists."

"Or the Quakers," Colonel Botfield shouted. "They'll listen to your braying cant!"

"It's you who need to hear the Lord's will," Reverend Greenberry proclaimed. But his voice shook, and he was mighty pale. If he hadn't had the lectern to hang on to, I think he'd have fallen to the floor in a dead faint.

Uncle Philemon rose to his feet. "I ain't trusting no Yankee to tell me the will of God Almighty," he roared.

With that, he shoved me out of the pew ahead of him and started for the door. Most of the congregation followed us.

"That's the last time I go to church," Uncle Philemon said when we got outside. "Never liked that fool's sermons anyway."

Normally I didn't care much for church myself. Reverend Greenberry had a way of droning on and on till the whole congregation fell asleep and had to be waked by a peal from the organ. But today he'd been a sight more interesting. Not one single person had so much as closed an eye during his sermon. Though I didn't dare say it, I halfway admired him for speaking his piece so boldly. But I still wasn't sure about Mr. Lincoln's notions being the Lord's will.

Church had given Uncle Philemon such a powerful thirst he took himself off to the tavern, leaving me to walk home alone. The road led past Miss Sally's house, so I stopped to see how Perry was. The old lady must have been watching for me. Before I had time to knock, she opened the door and beckoned me inside.

"I was hoping you'd come soon. The colonel's been by again. This time he stopped and asked me if I'd seen Lydia and the boy. I told him no, but I'm not sure he believed me. I'm scared he'll come with his dogs next time."

I looked around, but I didn't see a sign of Perry. Before I could ask, Miss Sally told me he was in the fruit cellar. "It's safer down there."

"How's he feeling?"

"Poorly. He misses his mama something fierce, plus he's got a touch of fever. You want to pay him a little visit?"

Miss Sally went to a corner of the room and rolled back a rag rug hiding a trapdoor. I followed her down the steep steps to the cellar. In the light of a lantern, I saw Perry lying on a cot, his back to the room. Miss Sally patted his shoulder. "Hey," she whispered, "Here's your friend Jesse come to see how you are."

Perry didn't move. "He's not my friend, and I don't

want to see him," he muttered. "Tell him to go away."

Miss Sally sat down beside him. "Now, Perry, what did we talk about this morning?"

"Going to Baltimore on the boat."

"And who's going with you?"

"Nobody. I'm going by myself."

Miss Sally sighed and beckoned me closer. "Sit up now, Perry, and talk to Jesse like a good boy. He's put himself at risk for you. The least you can do is show him some courtesy."

Perry rolled over and faced me, but he didn't sit up and he didn't smile and he didn't show any signs of courtesy. "I don't need him to take me to Baltimore. I can get there on my own."

Though I was trying to be patient, Perry was just too contrary for me to hold my tongue. "You ain't old enough to go to Baltimore by yourself. Why, I bet you don't even know where it is."

"It's across the Bay, up north," Perry said, but I could tell he had no notion which way north was.

"If you ain't the most ignorant boy—" I began but Miss Sally hushed me with a sharp look.

"You heard what your mama said," Miss Sally told Perry. "It was her wish that Jesse take you. He'll keep you safe."

Perry scowled but said nothing. From the look on his face, I reckoned he didn't believe I could keep myself safe, let alone anybody else. Maybe he was right to think so.

Miss Sally frowned. "You'd best get used to the idea, Perry. Jesse is taking you to Baltimore, and that's that."

Perry turned his back to us again. I had a feeling he'd started crying. Missing his mama, I reckoned. I knew how he felt, but I kept quiet. He didn't want comforting. Not from me at least.

Giving up on Perry, Miss Sally told me she'd made arrangements with her brother, Captain William Harrison. "He expects you on board his boat before his crew arrives. Come here around midnight on Thursday, and I'll have Perry ready."

She led me back to the kitchen and hid the trapdoor under the rug. "Don't let the child upset you," she said. "He's taking his mama's death real bad. Sometimes I think he blames us both for losing her."

I didn't say nothing, but Miss Sally's notions seemed daft to me. Let Perry blame the Widow Baxter, let him blame the colonel, let him blame the recently departed Mr. Peregrine Baxter. They were the ones who'd caused all the trouble. Not me or Miss Sally. In fact, it was downright rude of Perry to blame me just because I was handy and the true villains weren't.

"You don't care for the child, do you?" Miss Sally peered into my eyes, seeking the truth.

"He puts on airs," I muttered, "and he talks fancy. Why, he speaks better than me and he's a slave. Don't seem natural somehow."

Miss Sally sighed. "I don't approve of Mr. Peregrine Baxter's behavior, but he must have cared some for

Perry or he wouldn't have took the time to teach him to speak like a gentleman."

Somehow that didn't make Perry any better. Nobody had ever cared enough for me to teach me much of anything. Not that I wanted to learn. But still it rankled me somehow to think of that child knowing more of the King's English than I did.

"Jesse, for goodness sake," Miss Sally said. "Don't stand there pouting. Suppose your face freezes like that?" She gave me a little shake. "Just thank your stars Abednego Botfield ain't searching for you."

There was some truth to what she said, but it seemed likely the colonel might be searching for me as well as Perry one of these days. Anyways, I straightened up a bit and tried to change the look on my face.

"That's better," Miss Sally said. "You just remember what Perry's been through, losing his mama and that little baby and now going off to Baltimore with a boy he barely knows. His troubles aren't over, not by a long shot."

I wanted to say my troubles weren't over either, but it made no sense to keep on arguing.

Miss Sally gave me a little hug and told me to go on home. "Stay away from here till Thursday night," she said. "The colonel's most likely watching the house."

The way Perry acted, I would have liked to stay away forever, but I'd made a promise and I meant to keep it.

———————

The days of the week slid past quicker than I'd thought they would. Morning and night, raggedy V's of Canada geese flew overhead, baying like hounds. The trees put out little gold leaves, and the robins came back, but the weather stayed cold and gray.

News of the war kept Uncle Philemon in a constant uproar. First, we heard the federal army had surrendered Fort Sumter to the rebels without a single soul dying, which my uncle claimed was evidence Yankees were cowards to the core. Then Mr. Abraham Lincoln did just what my uncle predicted. He called up an army. Wanted 75,000 men to volunteer to quell the Confederates.

Worse yet, Mr. Lincoln aimed to send his army to South Carolina on the train. Boston, New York, Philadelphia—no matter where the train started up north, it couldn't go south without going through Baltimore.

"An invasion, that's what it is," Uncle Philemon hollered.

How could it be an invasion, I wondered, seeing as how Baltimore was in the United States of America same as those northern cities, but I didn't dare ask. Uncle Philemon was far too het up already.

"We have to secede now." Uncle Philemon pounded the table so hard he knocked his glass over and spilled a river of red wine across the white cloth. "Before the despot's heel grinds us into the dust!"

While Delia mopped up the wine, fussing to herself

in a low voice, I stared agape at Uncle Philemon. His face was so red I expected him to drop dead of apoplexy right in front of my eyes.

"Ain't you heard what's happened?" he asked me. "A passel of Mr. Lincoln's Yankees from Pennsylvania passed right through Baltimore on their way south today. Maryland can't put up with that!"

He gulped a mouthful of wine from the glass Delia had refilled. "They're expecting more Yankee troops on Friday. By God, I'd give a million dollars to be in Baltimore. I'd teach those pusillanimous pups a lesson!"

"Good thing you ain't got that kind of money," Delia muttered. "You'd get your fool head blown off for sure."

Uncle Philemon belched and glanced around to see if we'd noticed. Delia and I acted as if we hadn't heard a thing, so he cleared his throat and went on with his tirade about states' rights and Mr. Lincoln and the Yankees, abolitionists, and other villains seeking to ruin the nation.

Neither Delia nor I listened to a word he said. She went about her business serving food and I ate it, but I didn't much enjoy it. I couldn't help worrying about what might happen Friday, the very day I was supposed to take Perry to Baltimore.

CHAPTER 6

Thursday night, just after the clock struck midnight, I crept out the door. A couple of hounds came along with me. I reckoned they smelled the food I'd stuffed in my pockets, but they lost interest before I reached the road. They probably caught a whiff of coon or fox, because they took off toward the woods, and I saw no more of them. Which was just as well. Uncle Philemon would have been a sight more upset to lose those hounds than me.

I sneaked around to the back of Miss Sally's house and knocked on the door real soft. She opened it right away, like she'd been waiting with her hand on the knob. Perry was sitting in the rocking chair staring at me, his face closed up tight as a fist.

Miss Sally put her arms around him and held him tight, but the expression on his face didn't change. "You must go with Jesse now," she told him. "I'd keep you with me if I could, darling, but it's too dangerous here." She let him loose slowly and wiped her eyes with her apron.

"I told you I don't want to go with that boy," Perry muttered.

"You think I like you any better than you like me?" I asked, feeling ugly toward him.

Miss Sally hushed us. "Boys," she said, "you must be friends, you must help one another. Once you leave William's ship, you'll be among godless men for sure."

Pulling us together, she commenced to pray loudly for our safety and our brotherhood. "Believe me," she ended, "you'll never be out of the good Lord's sight. He'll be holding you both in the palm of His hand."

Though I kept my thoughts to myself, I hoped the Lord would keep a better grip on Perry and me than he'd kept on many another person I could name. Lydia, for one; Mama, for another. He had surely let them slip away into the darkness without paying any heed.

Perry didn't come fast or even willingly, but at least he allowed me to accompany him to Captain Harrison's dock. When we got in sight of the *Sally H.*'s masts, we hid in the tall marsh grass and studied the scene. Nothing seemed amiss. No strangers about, no horses.

But just as I stepped out of the shadows, Captain Harrison appeared on the ship's deck and held his hand up. "Get back," he whispered. "Somebody's coming."

We hunkered down in a clump of tall grass as quick and quiet as foxes. A few seconds later, Colonel Abednego Botfield rode out of the dark like some cussed nightmare, the kind you have over and over again till you're scared to go to sleep. I was beginning to think that my fate, whatever it was, was somehow tied up with that villain.

Not ten feet away, the colonel stopped his horse and hollered for Captain Harrison. His voice rang across the black water like Satan summoning his troops from hell.

Captain Harrison leaned over the boat's railing to have a look at Colonel Botfield. "Why, Abednego," he said, sounding a heap more cheerful than he must have felt. "What brings you here in the middle of the night?"

"I need passage to Baltimore," Colonel Botfield said. "I understand you're shipping a load of fish to market before sunup. How about taking me along?"

Captain Harrison paused a second. "Why, I don't believe I can do that," he said slowly. "I have my crew and a hold full of rockfish. There's no room for anyone else. Wouldn't be safe."

"I can pay you a handsome fee," Colonel Botfield said.

"I'm sorry, Abednego, but I can't take the risk no matter what you're willing to pay." Captain Harrison managed to sound truly apologetic.

Colonel Botfield swore a long string of cuss words. "I tell you, it's imperative I get to Baltimore."

"And I tell you, I can't take you," Captain Harrison said, no longer sounding a bit sorry. I reckoned hearing those cuss words riled him something terrible. Methodists just don't tolerate that kind of talk.

Colonel Botfield cursed again and wheeled his

horse around so fast the big bay's hooves scattered bits of oyster shells in all directions. "I'll find someone else, William Harrison," he shouted. "And when I arrive in Baltimore, I won't smell like a stinking fish."

With that, the man galloped off the way he'd come, passing so close we heard him swear as he rode by.

A few minutes later, Captain Harrison called to us, and we hurried aboard the *Sally H.* I looked back once, to make sure Colonel Botfield was truly gone. The road was empty, the night dark, the stars high in the heavens. For now, at least, we were safe from the villain. I wished, hoped, and prayed he wouldn't find his way to Baltimore, for if he did, I had no doubt he'd find us.

Captain Harrison hid us in the boat's dinghy on the stern. He'd lined the small boat with some of Miss Sally's quilts and made sure we had water and food. "Stay put till we reach Baltimore. I don't want my crew to see you."

So saying, he covered the dinghy with a canvas and went on about his business.

Somehow the two of us managed to fall asleep, or at least I did. Perry was so quiet, who knows whether he slept or not? Maybe he just lay there all night, staring into the dark and thinking the Lord knows what.

When I woke up and saw the tarpaulin over my head, I thought I'd been buried alive. If Perry hadn't sighed in his sleep, I'd have started hollering for help, but as soon as I saw him, I remembered where we were. The boat was moving, I could feel the rock and sway of it, and there was enough light seeping through the tarpaulin to tell me it was early morning.

I had to pee something awful so I used the little pail Captain Harrison had left for that purpose. Then I eased the tarp back and peered out. In the dim dawn light I saw the captain standing at the wheel, his back to me. A man I knew, Daniel Wrightson, swabbed the deck a few feet away. Two or three other fellows busied themselves with their tasks. None of them looked my way.

Taking a quick glance at the water and the sky, I saw farmland and trees and one small town with docks poking into the Bay like wooden fingers and boats as small as toys bobbing on the water. I couldn't tell if I was looking at the western shore or the eastern shore. All I knew was we were somewhere on the Chesapeake Bay between Talbot County and Baltimore.

As I dropped the tarp, I glanced at Perry. He lay on his back, eyes wide open, staring at me.

"Hey," I whispered. "You feel all right?"

Perry said nothing, didn't even nod his head. Just looked at me as if he hated me too much to waste his breath talking.

"You want something to eat?" I showed him the biscuits and cheese Miss Sally had given us.

He made no response. Feeling irked, I told myself he was missing his mama something terrible. Maybe it had nothing to do with me at all. Maybe he was just too sad to talk.

"How about a drink of water?" I asked, trying to be patient. "Ain't you thirsty?"

Still nothing.

"Maybe you need to pee." I pointed at the bucket, which was already beginning to scent the air under the tarp. "You can use that."

When he was done with the bucket, I ate my share of the biscuits and cheese. Perry watched like he'd forgotten what eating was and had no interest in remembering.

"Come on," I begged, waving a biscuit under his nose. "You need to eat. You'll get too weak to walk."

Perry kept his mouth shut so tight it might have been drawn on his face with a pencil.

"Listen here," I said, running out of patience with him. "You ain't the first child in this world to lose your mama. My own mama died when I was younger than you, and my daddy died soon after. I still feel mighty bad about it, but I don't go round making everybody else miserable."

Perry looked at me as if my loss had no bearing on his own misery. "It's not the same," he said. "You have kin to care for you. You're not all alone in the world like me." Tears filled his eyes and ran down his cheeks.

"You got kin, Perry. That's why we're going to Baltimore. Remember? Your mama wants you to be with your aunt Polly, your daddy's very own sister."

Perry scowled at me through his tears. "What if she gives me back to the Widow?"

"Why on earth would she do that?"

He gave me a look that clearly said I was too stupid to put one foot in front of the other. "I'm not white like her, am I?" Then, without saying another word, he turned away and curled up into a little ball.

I stared at his back. It was true that some white folks scorned their black kin, but others treated them real good. I figured Lydia knew Polly a sight better than Perry did. If she trusted Polly, then I trusted Polly, too.

Weary of arguing with the child, I set the food down beside him. "There it is," I said. "Your share. Take it or leave it." I lay back and closed my eyes. My stomach rose and fell with the boat, and I wished I hadn't eaten so much. Hoping to feel better, I let the motion rock me back to sleep.

The next time I woke, I could tell by the noise and commotion we'd docked. The crew was unloading the fish, shouting and calling to each other to mind this and watch that. Perry was awake, too. I noticed he'd eaten his food.

Captain Harrison had told us not to show ourselves till he said it was safe, so we stayed in the dinghy and waited. It was hot and stuffy and the bucketful of pee stunk like an outhouse in desperate need of lime. Though Perry didn't so much as wrinkle his nose, I was busting my britches to breathe some fresh air.

At last Captain Harrison poked his face under the tarpaulin. "You can come out now, boys," he said. "And dump that bucket overboard. I swear, it reeks to high heaven."

After I'd done as he said, I stood on the deck of the *Sally H.* and stared at the harbor. Never had I seen anything like Baltimore City. Ships of all sizes and kinds rocked on the water—steamboats with tall stacks and paddlewheels, old schooners, sloops, barges, and I don't know what all. Some were from foreign places, China, England, Holland, India. Their names were painted on the prows in strange writing with curlicued letters, and they flew flags I'd never seen before. Others were as American as the *Sally H.*

The ships' decks swarmed with crews loading and unloading everything from fish to tea and silk. They called out to one another in languages I'd never heard. The whole world seemed to be right here in Baltimore. Why, the very air smelled like spice with a tang of dead fish and salty water mixed in.

Beyond the harbor, tall, skinny houses crowded together, row after row of them, climbing uphill from the water. Their rooftops and chimneys stretched toward the sky. Here and there church steeples poked up, higher than everything else, pointing the way to heaven. Closer to the ground was a jumble of waterfront taverns. Most likely that was as far as Uncle Philemon got on his visits to Baltimore.

Somewhere amongst all those buildings was the house where Miss Polly Baxter lived. I hoped with all my heart to get Perry there safely and be back to the Shore before my uncle even noticed I was gone.

CHAPTER 7

Captain Harrison tapped my shoulder to get my attention. "Where are you taking the boy?"

"Number 115 West Monument Street," I told him.

"That's not too far from here." He thought a second or two and told me the way. "Just be sure and aim for the Washington Monument at the top of the hill on Charles Street," he finished up. "West Monument Street will be to your left."

It seemed a long way to walk with a runaway slave, but Captain Harrison said nobody would pay Perry any mind. "If they ask," he added, "just say your daddy owns him."

"Nobody owns me," Perry spoke up for the first time all morning. "If you say anyone does, I'll call you a liar, Jesse Sherman."

"That's the right spirit," Captain Harrison said, "but sometimes you have to lie to protect yourself, Perry. You can't go around announcing to the world you're a runaway. Got to show some sense."

Perry frowned and jammed his hands deep in his pockets. The captain turned his head and spat overboard into the thick brown water. The Bay was a sight dirtier here in Baltimore. I saw a rat floating belly up, keeping company with a mess of dead fish, rotten fruit, bottles, broken crates and barrels, all washing against the sides of the *Sally H*.

Captain Harrison laid his hand on my shoulder. "Be careful, Jesse. The city's in an ugly mood today. Got something to do with Union troops coming through on their way south. Looks like trouble."

Perry paid no mind to this, but I remembered what Uncle Philemon had said. "What kind of trouble?" I asked.

The captain shook his head. "All I can say is keep your wits about you. If anything goes wrong, I can't wait on you. My crew expects to be home tonight."

Before we left the wharf, I looked back at the *Sally H*. Captain Harrison was watching us from the deck, his face worried. "Remember what I said," he called. "Get back to the boat before dark."

With Perry beside me, I led the way up Fell Street. It seemed like everyone was out and about, rushing here and there, pushing and yelling. Women as well as men, blacks as well as white, free men as well as slaves, all going about their business. Some sold wares, shouting out what they had—fish and crabs, mostly. Others shouted what they could do for you—mend your pots, sharpen your knives, pull your teeth, cure your ills.

Nobody paid Perry and me any notice. To keep from being shoved into the street, we edged along close to the houses, dodging doorsteps and trash. So far I'd seen nothing to make me like Baltimore. I could scarcely wait to get back to the Shore and breathe fresh air again.

As we passed a tavern, three men barged out the door and nearly knocked us flat. "Those Yankee soldiers ain't coming through Baltimore," one of them yelled.

"No, sir, just let 'em try," another hollered and waved a South Carolina flag.

At the same moment, a gang of rough-looking sailors and roustabouts surged past us. Some were carrying clubs and bottles. One brandished a harpoon. Others had rocks in their hands. They were shouting and swearing about Mr. Lincoln's army, too.

Another mob poured out of a tavern across the street. "To the train station," a big red-faced man shouted. "That's where the Yankees are. Come on, boys, let's bust some heads!"

Perry and I pressed ourselves against a building and watched them go by. Though I tried to hide it, I was scared. The men were looking for a fight, any fool could see that. And drunk, too, from the smell of them. Like the captain had said, trouble was brewing for sure.

On Lancaster Street, the crowd was bigger. The men were all going the same way, and we were carried along with them like bits of wood in a flooded river.

Though Perry didn't have nothing to say, he kept close to my side without me telling him to. I reckoned he realized it was a good thing he had company.

At the President Street Station, we were stopped by a team of horses trying to pull train cars full of Yankee soldiers along a track running right down the middle of the road. I don't know where the locomotive was. Maybe it was busted.

But whatever the cause, the soldiers were in a bad situation. All around them, men were tearing up cobblestones and hurling them and whatever else they could grab at the cars. Train windows shattered. The Yankees inside ducked and swore. The horses pulling the cars whinnied and reared up.

A bunch of roustabouts dragged anchors and timbers from the wharves and shoved them on the tracks. Gunshots rang out here and there. People cursed the Union and Mr. Lincoln both. A skinny man in a shabby frock coat waved the South Carolina flag and cheered for the rebels.

It was a good thing my uncle wasn't there. Delia was right. He'd have got himself killed in no time.

"Down with the Yankee hirelings!" a man near me yelled.

"Give me some gunpowder," another cried. "I'll blow 'em to kingdom come!"

Yet another ripped open his shirt and bared his chest. "Shoot me," he screamed at the soldiers, "I dare you!"

I tried to find a way out of the crowd, but everybody was big and mad. They pushed us this way and shoved us that way. I was scared we'd end up trampled underfoot.

The farther we went, the worse the rioting got. By now the soldiers had abandoned the train cars. They were marching down the middle of the street, pressed tight together, carrying their guns over their shoulders as if they were in a parade. Some looked scared. Others looked angry. Most just stepped along grim-faced, trying hard to ignore the rotten vegetables a crowd of women was hurling at them.

The man with the South Carolina flag managed to get in front of the soldiers. He strutted along ahead, grinning like it was a good joke to force the Yankees to march behind a rebel flag. Folks in the crowd cheered at the sight.

Around this time a man someone identified as the mayor of Baltimore thrust himself into the line of soldiers and started marching with them. I reckon he thought the sight of him would have some effect on matters, but things just went from bad to worse.

Every intersection was blocked with sawhorses, wagons, anchors from the harbor, and anything else handy. On Pratt Street, people were throwing things at the Yankees from windows and rooftops—stones, bricks, bottles, pitchers, chairs. A walnut bureau plummeted down and splintered to bits at my feet. The noise scared Perry and me both. Neither of us had ever been in a crowd like this, nor had we ever seen so many people.

By now Baltimore's fine citizens had begun shooting at the soldiers from porches and open windows. Every now and then the Yankees fired back but the mob pressed so tight around them they could scarcely raise their guns. Just ahead of me, I saw a soldier go down, his chest spurting blood. I'd seen deer killed, I'd shot a heap of muskrats, rabbits, and squirrels myself, but I'd never seen a man shot. I tried to back up so as not to step on him, but the mob pushed me right over him.

Suddenly a strong bony hand grasped my shoulder, and I heard a voice I'd hoped never to hear again. "Well, well," Colonel Botfield said. "We meet once more, Jesse Sherman."

The Colonel's nails bit into my skin as if he had claws on the ends of his fingers. "It appears you've got part of what I'm looking for," he said, grabbing Perry's arm. "But where's his mama?"

While Perry and I struggled to escape, the crowd roared and surged around us, pushing us out to its edges and finally pressing the three of us up against a wall. No one paid the least notice. Perry and I might as well have been in the middle of a barren desert for all the help we got.

Colonel Botfield tightened his grip on me till my arm tingled all the way down to my fingertips. The pain was fearsome. "No more fooling," he said. "Where's Lydia?"

"With the good Lord and all his saints," I gasped, trying to keep a grip on Perry with my free hand. "Safe from you forever."

"Lydia's dead?" Colonel Botfield stared at me, as if sorely grieved to hear he'd lost the reward money. "How did she die?"

"Birthing a baby down in the marsh." I glared at the man with all the hatred in my soul. "Where she went to hide from you and the widow."

For a moment the colonel acted as if he didn't know what to say or do. He just stood there cursing with half of Baltimore surging around us, screaming and hollering. "Where is she?" he demanded. "What did you do with her?"

I reckoned the old villain was fixing to dig up the body and take it to the Widow Baxter, still hoping to get his hands on that hundred-dollar reward. "She's buried someplace you'll never find her," I yelled.

For that I got a crack across the mouth hard enough to draw blood. "Go back home, Jesse," the colonel drawled, "before you get your sorry self killed."

Shoving me aside, he tightened his grip on Perry, who'd been hollering the whole while, kicking and flailing his fists and matching the colonel's profanity word for word. "Come with me, boy," he snarled. "Your mama might be dead, but you're still alive."

"I won't let you have him!" I grabbed at Perry, catching hold of his shirt. "You got no claim to him!"

"Believe me, I got more claim than you do." The

colonel jerked at Perry, tearing his shirt out of my hands.

The boy sunk his teeth in the old devil's arm, but neither he nor I was any match for Colonel Botfield. The next thing I knew, he'd struck me again, knocking me to my knees this time. He took off with Perry, and I ran after him, ducking the rocks and bottles meant for the soldiers. A stone hit my shoulder, a bullet whizzed over my head, but I finally got close enough to catch hold of Colonel Botfield's coattails.

"Give him back," I cried. "I'll get money, I'll pay you for him, just don't take him!"

Perry reached for me, but Colonel Botfield eyed me with scorn. "You vex me, boy." With no warning, he pulled out a pistol and struck me hard on the side of the head.

Stunned, I fell flat in the street. For a second or two, I rolled this way and that, ducking the hobnailed boots pounding the pavement all around me. When I finally scrambled to my feet, dazed and bleeding, Colonel Abednego Botfield had disappeared like the devil he was. Gone straight down to hell, for all I knew, taking Perry with him.

A hole opened in the crowd and I half staggered, half fell into an alley. Blood streamed down my face, blinding me. My head felt like it was split in half. Sprawled among rotten fish and vegetables, I began to cry. Between sobs, I cursed Colonel Abednego Botfield, I cursed Baltimore City, I cursed myself for being a stupid boy.

While I lay in the filth bawling, the sounds from the street slowly faded. The hollering stopped. The shooting stopped. The riot had finally burned itself out like a forest fire.

When I was sure it was safe, I ventured to the end of the alley and peered up and down Pratt Street. I was so dizzy I could hardly stand, but at least my head had stopped bleeding.

All around me, wounded men groaned in the gutters. Torn knapsacks and bedrolls were strewn everywhere, along with bricks, broken bottles, and smashed furniture. There was blood, too, whole puddles of it. And, worst of all, just a few feet away, a man lay on the pavement, his arms outflung, his face white and drawn, his eyes wide open. He was the same fellow I'd seen near the station earlier, daring a soldier to shoot him. It seemed someone had done as he asked.

I'd never seen a battlefield, but I reckoned this was how one looked after the fighting was over. I threw up then and there, emptying my stomach of everything I'd eaten on the *Sally H.* that morning.

A couple of men carried another body past on a stretcher. They didn't pay no mind to me. Just trudged along carrying that bloody corpse.

One said to the other, "I hear ten Yankees got killed today."

"I heard it was twice that many. Maybe more."

"How many civilians?"

"Ten or twelve, somebody said."

"Damn Federals." The man spit in the gutter. "Firing on unarmed folks. Seems to me they ought to be hanged for that."

After the men rounded a corner, I sagged against the wall, sunk in misery. I yearned to run back to the ship and tell Captain Harrison I'd done all I could for Perry. He'd take me home, and that would be the end of it.

But of course it wouldn't be the end of it. Once something like this got started, it didn't quit till it was done. And that wouldn't be till Perry was safe.

There was nothing for me to do but go to that house on Monument Street and find Miss Polly Baxter. Even though he was a slave, Perry was her nephew and a pretty child at that. Surely she'd help get him back from Colonel Abednego Botfield.

CHAPTER 8

I staggered uphill on Charles Street, reeling this way and that like Uncle Philemon coming home from the tavern. Way far ahead I could see a statue of George Washington standing on top of a tall column, gazing out over the city. Trouble was, I was so dizzy I saw two of everything, including the monument itself. My knees felt like they'd melted. And I kept vomiting, though there was nothing in my belly but green stuff that burned my throat when it came up.

Somehow I made my way to that tall column and from thence to number 115 West Monument Street. It was a grand place, well kept and dignified, the home of ladies and gentlemen. Here I was, dirty and bloody and so dizzy I could scarcely stand up. How was I to knock on that big door and ask for Miss Polly Baxter? Why, she'd never speak to a raggedy boy like me.

While I stood there, swaying back and forth, the

door opened and out came a well-dressed gent wearing a black armband. I had to stare hard to keep from seeing two of him. "Come along, step lively, don't dawdle," he called to someone inside.

A plumpish woman hastened out the door, followed by a pretty young lady with a melancholy look. Both were dressed in black silk dresses. Maybe it was the color of their clothing, but the two of them were as pale as pale could be. Behind them came a young Negro woman, toting more boxes than she could manage.

I guessed the pale young lady to be Miss Polly Baxter, but before I dared say a word to her, a carriage drove up. In a trice, they all climbed inside and went rattling away down Monument Street.

"Hey, what are you doing hanging around here, boy?"

I wheeled and found myself face to face with a large Negro woman about the age of Delia. She was standing in the doorway of number 115, broom in hand, getting ready to sweep me away with the rest of the dirt.

I reckon I'd turned too fast, for all of a sudden I got so dizzy I couldn't see straight. The woman turned into a pair of twins, everything went as black as those silk dresses, and I felt myself falling, falling, falling. The last thing I heard was the woman saying, "What's wrong, wrong, wrong . . ." and then I was gone into the dark.

For a long while after that, I passed in and out of strange dreams and visions. In one, the wind blew me higher and higher, way above the roofs of Baltimore and on across the Bay, all the way back to the little house where I was born, and there was Mama alive and well and so happy to see me. All those other babies were there, too, laughing and gay, as healthy as children could be. Through the window I saw Daddy plowing the field, strong the way he was before he sickened.

I put my arms around Mama and held her tight and smelled her sweet smell. I wanted to ask where she'd been all this time, but I knew not to. Such a question would break the spell.

Then Lydia stepped through the door, carrying her baby girl, the one that died, only she was alive now and smiling at me. Lydia came over to Mama and touched her arm. "You can't keep him here," she said. "He's got promises to keep."

Mama held me tighter, and then ever so gently she loosed herself from my arms. "You must go back, son," she whispered. "It's not your time to join me."

"No, don't make me go, Mama. Let me stay with you."

But Lydia came between us. "Remember your promise, Jesse. Find Perry and get him to Polly, so I can rest peaceful."

In a flash, she and Mama and all the others were gone and I was alone in a dark, narrow street. Somehow I knew I was in Baltimore, just outside Slattery's slave jail. I heard sounds of misery from behind the wall, cries and sobs and groans, wails and shrieks mixed with hollering and cursing and whips cracking. Out of the shadows stepped Colonel Abednego Botfield, taller than life, his eyes glowing red as a hellhound's. In one hand he held a pistol, pointed at my heart. His other hand gripped Perry.

"This boy is mine," Colonel Botfield snarled. "You'll never get him."

Behind me stood Lydia, knife at my throat. "You promised to keep him safe," she hissed in my ear. "You swore on my grave!"

Just as Colonel Botfield pulled the trigger, everything changed, and I was all alone again in a strange place, crying for Mama.

"There now, there now," someone said softly. "Rest easy, boy."

I opened my eyes to find myself lying on a straw pallet in a small dark room lit only by a candle. The ceiling was low and the air smelled of mold and dust. At first I thought I was in a jail cell, but just as I was about to holler in fright, a Negro woman leaned over and patted my hand.

I tried to ask her who she was and where I was, but my throat was sore and my mouth was dry and my voice was no more than a croak.

"Hush," the woman said. "You been mighty sick. First there was your head. You lost a lot of blood and nearly died from a concussion. Then the fever set in."

She pressed a cool cloth against my head. "Goodness gracious, boy, you've kept me on my knees for more than two weeks praying the Lord to spare your young life."

"Two weeks?" I tried to sit up but found I couldn't manage it. The fever had left me weak as a baby. "I have to find Perry, I promised his mama I'd take care of him, I—"

"Lie still, and drink this." The woman held a cup of something hot to my lips. It smelled like swamp water and I shut my mouth tight, recalling some of Delia's medical concoctions. They tasted so bad a body got well just to save himself from drinking them.

"Come on, honey," the woman coaxed. "Take a few swallows, like a good boy." She pushed the cup firmly against my lips until she managed to get a few drops into my mouth. It tasted just as bad as it smelled, but I swallowed it anyway. Which encouraged her to pour more into me.

"My name's Athena," she went on. "You been here at Judge Baxter's home since I found you, off your head most of the time, shouting all sorts of nonsense about some child and Miss Polly—"

"Please go fetch Miss Polly Baxter," I cut in. "I got news from her dear friend Lydia. And Perry—I have to tell her about Perry." Shaking with worry, I clutched Athena's hand.

Athena stared at me, her face full of distrust. "How do you know Miss Polly? Who are you anyway, boy? Where do you come from?"

I told Athena my name, and then I let the whole

story tumble out. How Lydia caught me in the woods and made me promise to bring Perry to Miss Polly Baxter. How the poor young woman birthed a dead baby and then died herself. How Miss Sally and I buried her and the baby in the woods. How Perry and I came to Baltimore on Captain Harrison's ship.

I didn't leave nothing out. Not even the part about the late Mr. Peregrine Baxter being Perry's father. By the time I came to Colonel Abednego Botfield, I was sniffling and snuffling and biting my lip to keep from crying.

"I promised Lydia I'd keep her boy safe," I finished up, all hoarse and tearful. "I swore on her very grave, and now the colonel has him."

"Lord, Lord, it grieves my heart to hear tell of Lydia's death." Athena left off stroking my forehead and stared into the shadows. "The judge used to take me along when the family visited Mr. Peregrine and Mrs. Henrietta," she went on. "Miss Polly always sought Lydia out. They was the same age, you know. They used to chatter together out on the lawn like a pair of pretty birds."

Athena paused like she was thinking hard. "I don't believe Lydia ever told Miss Polly about having a child with Mr. Peregrine. I never knew it myself. Lydia must have kept that boy hidden away when we visited." She sighed and wiped her eyes. "Do you have any notion where the colonel might have taken the child?"

"The Widow Baxter wanted both Lydia and Perry sold south at Slattery's slave jail," I said. "I reckon that's exactly where the colonel took Perry. He could be anywhere now. Mississippi, Louisiana. I'll never find him, never."

I busted out crying in earnest, which shamed me nearly as much as losing Perry. I had to get up and find him or die trying, but I didn't have the strength even to push the bedcovers back. "Please tell Miss Polly I got a message for her," I begged Athena. "Let me explain things to her. Surely she'll help me find Perry."

"Oh, Jesse, I'm sad to say Miss Polly's not here," Athena said slowly. "On the very day you showed up, Judge Baxter sent her and his wife to his brother's place in the country. The city's in such an uproar, with some folks wanting to join the rebels and others wanting to stay in the Union, he didn't think they was safe."

Hearing that, I knew what people meant when they said their hearts sank. Mine plummeted like a rock down to the very bottom of a deep, dark well. Perry lost, Miss Polly Baxter gone, and me as weak as a baby— what was I to do now?

I reckon Athena guessed how I was feeling, for she fixed her dark eyes on me and said, "Don't you fret, Jesse. When you get your strength back, I'll help you find that little boy of Lydia's."

I lay back, too weary to speak another word. In my weak state, I even let Athena pour more of her swamp water down my throat. For a while the only sound was the rain tapping against a tiny window up near the ceiling.

"Sleep now," Athena said. "And don't go blaming

yourself for what's happened. You done your best to help that child."

She went to the door but turned back to say, "You're in the slave quarters. No one's sleeping down here but me and Nate, the judge's man. Hyacinth went to the country with Miss Polly and her mother." She paused as someone walked across the floor over our heads. "Be as quiet as you can, Jesse. That's the judge pacing around up there. I don't want him to know you're here. He ain't a bad man, just a mite short on charity."

After Athena left, I was all alone in the dark. Though I meant to stay awake, my eyelids grew so heavy I soon gave up and drifted back into dreams I didn't want to dream. In some I was burying Perry in a deep hole in the woods beside his mama. In others, I was ducking bullets from the colonel's pistol. In the worst ones, Lydia came after me with that big sharp knife of hers, threatening to kill me for breaking my sacred vow.

I feared I'd never get a good night's sleep again, not with dreams like mine.

CHAPTER 9

I don't know how long I lay on that pallet in the cellar. The sun never shone through the little window, but sometimes the light was gray and I knew it was daytime. Other times it was black and I knew it was night. But mostly day and night ran together in a blur of fever dreams.

Athena came and went, bringing me food and her swamp water concoctions. Slowly I got stronger. First I could sit up, then I could totter around. I was like a baby learning how to do things all over again.

One morning I decided I was strong enough to go upstairs and see if Athena might let me start hunting for Perry. The more time went by, the less chance I had of finding him. I waited till I was sure the judge had left for the courthouse, and then I tiptoed up the steps. My legs shook a little, but I figured they'd bear my weight. Fresh air would do me good, too.

At the top of the stairs I stopped and listened. I could hear Athena laughing and talking with a man, his deep voice rumbling. I peered through the doorway to see who was with her. A young Negro man sat at the kitchen table, drinking coffee. I guessed him to be Nate, the judge's man Athena had told me about.

I figured it was safe to join them, but when I stepped through the door, Nate stopped in the middle of a sentence and stared at me, his face as sober as a preacher's.

"Is that the boy you been tending to?" he asked Athena.

She nodded, her smile gone, too. "Like I said, Nate, Jesse's a good boy. He won't cause us no trouble." She motioned me to sit down and went to fix me a bowl of oatmeal.

Nate watched her set the bowl in front of me. I was hoping he'd finish the funny story he'd been telling. After all I'd been through, I could have used a good laugh. But all he said was, "He looks like something the cat drug in, but that don't mean he won't bring us grief."

"Now, Nate," Athena said. "I told you why Jesse came here. He's trying to get Lydia's child back from Colonel Botfield."

Nate shook his head, but he didn't say nothing. Just sat there drinking his coffee while I tackled my oatmeal. Every now and then, he glanced at me like he was sizing me up. It was clear he had no use for me. Which hurt my feelings, for hadn't Athena just told him I was trying to keep a promise to a slave like himself? Surely he couldn't be thinking I was up to no good.

When I was done eating, I told Athena what was on my mind. "I can't wait no longer. I've got to find Perry."

Athena studied me as if I was a horse she was considering buying. She examined my eyes, my ears, and my throat. She even ran a finger across the raw red scar on my forehead.

"Just look at you," she muttered. "Skinny as a bean pole and whiter than cake flour. A gust of wind could blow you away like milkweed seeds."

"I've always been skinny, and I've always been pale," I said. "Besides, I made a promise, I told you I did, and I got to keep it."

Athena sighed. "You been here almost four weeks, Jesse. How do you expect to find that poor child now? There's no telling what's become of him."

"Just tell me where Slattery's slave jail is," I said. "I'll go down there and ask about Perry."

"If Mr. Slattery's got the boy," Athena said, "he's going to want money for him."

"Perry is Judge Baxter's grandson," I reminded her. "Surely he'd pay any price to get his own kin out of a place like that."

"If you have the sense you were born with," Athena said, "you'll keep your mouth shut about that."

Before I could think of a comeback, Nate spoke up.

"I'm done my work for today. I'll take Jesse down to Mr. Slattery's place. Might be good for him to see it."

Athena didn't look happy about this turn of events. "You be careful, Nate. A strong young man like you—somebody's likely to snatch you up and sell you south, too."

"Don't you worry none, Athena," Nate answered. "I'll take good care of the boy and myself, too. Besides we got Union soldiers all over the city now. Things are changing."

"Not fast enough," Athena muttered, but she went to the door with us. "Go down the alley to Centre Street," she told Nate. "You don't want the neighbors seeing you out and about like you ain't got nothing to do."

"I told you, I can take care of myself, Athena."

Nate led me outside and down a narrow alley to Centre Street. After all that time in the cellar, the bright sunlight made me squint. The city seemed bigger and noisier than I remembered. More crowded, too. I kept close to Nate, glad to be with someone his size.

On Charles Street, we stopped to watch a unit of Maryland soldiers march past. They looked right smart in their brand-new blue uniforms. A band led them, playing stirring songs. I spied a drummer boy no older than me, looking mighty pleased with himself.

Even though they were Yankees, the music made me want to run along behind them, following wherever they went, earning glory in battle like them. I reckon I'd have felt the same way if they'd been Confederates. It was the music that got to me more than anything else.

Most of the people on the street didn't give a fig for the music or the soldiers either. They jeered as the troops passed and called them traitors to the state of Maryland.

Among the crowd were three young ladies dressed in red and white gowns, sporting the Confederate stars and bars. "Look at that fellow carrying a ham," one girl laughed. "Why, it's bigger than he is!"

The little soldier just grinned and waved, but some of his companions hooted at the girls. It didn't seem to bother them none. They just drew closer together and giggled, swishing their silky skirts.

"Big brave Lincoln's lambs," the girls called.

The crowd guffawed and took up the name, chanting it till the soldiers turned down Pratt Street at the bottom of the hill.

Slowly the music faded away and the people went back to doing whatever they'd been doing before the soldiers came along. Still whispering and giggling, the three girls passed right by us and disappeared into a house on the corner.

Nate scowled. "Miss Polly's friends," he muttered. "Baltimore Belles, they call themselves. They're for the South, like their mamas and papas."

No matter what Nate thought, those girls were mighty pretty. Especially the one who'd cried out about the ham. Their dresses were fetching, too. I kept my opinion to myself, for I didn't want Nate to think I was for the South, too. Truth to tell, I hadn't made up my mind which army I'd join when I was old enough. But I couldn't help wondering a little about Miss Polly. If she agreed with her friends, how was she going to feel about Perry? It hurt my head to think about it, so I pushed the question away and hurried along with Nate, trying to match my step to his.

On we went, making our way downhill toward the harbor. By the time we got in sight of the slave jail's tall wooden gate, we were in the worst part of Baltimore I'd seen yet. Tumbledown old houses propped each other up, roofs sagging, paint peeling, windows busted. Mazes of muddy alleys and narrow rutted streets led off in all directions. Rats as big as cats sniffed the garbage. People in rags, their faces grimy, eyed Nate and me like they were wondering how much money we had. Luckily they decided we didn't have enough coins in our pockets to bother with.

Nate stopped on the corner about a block away from Slattery's. "I'd best wait here, Jesse. Like Athena said, some of them slave catchers will grab any Negro, slave or free."

I had no wish to enter that jail by myself, but I didn't want to put Nate in danger. Leaving him where he was, I followed a smartly dressed gent through the gate.

The first thing I saw was a group of white men crowded around a platform, pushing and shoving each other to get a better look at slaves chained to posts. Some of the Negroes held their heads up and stared at the crowd, but others sagged in their chains, their heads bowed, their bodies covered with cuts and bruises. I saw one or two that weren't much bigger than me, and I shuddered to think Perry might be here, bruised and bleeding and scared.

Behind the platform was a two-story building with barred windows. On the second floor, women pressed their faces against the bars. They waved their hands, they reached out, they cried the names of their husbands and sons, they wept. Some clutched little children to their breasts, their eyes wide with fear. Other shook the bars in rage and screamed at the crowd. It seemed hell was right here in Baltimore, and I hadn't even known it.

Paying no mind to the women, the men around the platform began yelling out bids for a tall black man. The seller, a scrawny white man, his narrow face pitted with pox scars, stripped off the slave's shirt to show his broad shoulders and muscles.

"This here's a mighty fine worker," he yelled to be heard above the racket. "Just look at him, strong as an ox."

"How did he come by them scars on his back?" a man hollered. "'Pears to me he's been whipped and whipped good. Might be his attitude is poor."

"Either that or he's a runaway," another fellow said.

"He's trouble for sure," the first man said. "I'll give you twenty dollars for him. Not a cent more."

"Now, listen here," the seller said, leaning closer to the crowd as if he had a good secret to share. "I got this man from Colonel Abednego Botfield, so you know I'm telling you God's own truth. He won't be no trouble. Not now." The seller laughed, showing a mouthful of yellow teeth worn down to stumps. "He's broke and broke for good."

I looked at the slave more closely. He'd been whipped all right, but he wasn't broke. Despite the chains on his wrists and ankles, any fool could see the fire smoldering in his eyes—fire no man, not even one as wicked as Colonel Abednego Botfield, could put out.

"What can I do for you, sonny?" I'd been staring at the slave so hard I hadn't noticed the man who now stood before me. Dressed in a black frock coat and striped trousers, he looked a gentleman, but he didn't fool me. No man of breeding would dirty his shoes in this place.

"I come to find a slave child Colonel Abednego Botfield brought here a while back," I said, hoping to sound braver than I felt. "A boy by the name of Perry, about seven or eight years old. Fair-skinned and pretty."

"The colonel never brought no child here." The man paused and gave me a long, hard look. "What's it to you, anyway?"

"Judge Baxter himself sent me to fetch him," I said, thinking fast. "The child belonged to his son, the late Mr. Peregrine Baxter. The colonel had no right to him."

The auctioneer came up to us and doffed his hat.

"Mr. Slattery, sir," he said, "the gent over there in the brown coat is doing his best to drive my prices down."

"I'll be with you in a minute, Jarvis. Don't be too particular, though. The way things are going, we got to take what we can get these days." Mr. Slattery spit on the cobblestones at my feet and scowled at me. "I don't know what you're up to, but it don't really matter, as I ain't got the boy."

Before I knew what he was up to, he shoved me so hard I fell into a puddle. "Get your sorry self out of here before I lose my temper," he sneered.

Jarvis laughed as I picked myself up. I didn't look at him or Mr. Slattery. Keeping my head up, I walked out of the slave jail as fast as I could, my heart pounding with the worst anger I'd ever felt.

Out in the street, I took a few deep breaths. Though it shocked me to think such thoughts, I wanted to whip Mr. Slattery and Jarvis till the skin peeled off their backs in strips, like they done the slaves. Maybe I'd even hang the villains. Then I'd free the slaves and burn the jail down. And Mr. Slattery with it. The devil would be happy to welcome him to hell. He probably already had places set aside for him and Colonel Botfield.

CHAPTER 10

Nate was standing where I'd left him, leaning against the wall of a shabby old house. "Did you find any trace of the child?"

Close to tears, I shook my head. "Mr. Slattery himself told me he don't have Perry. He claimed Colonel Botfield never brung him here." I looked at him in despair. "Oh, Nate, I never seen a place so hateful nor met a man worse than Mr. Slattery."

Nate looked down the street to the gates of the slave jail. "Won't be there much longer," he said. "Mr. Abraham Lincoln ain't one to tolerate such things in a Union state. He'll put Mr. Slattery and his kind out of business soon enough. You just see if he don't."

He reached for my arm. "Let's go along home now, Jesse. You look plain tuckered out."

I dug my heels into the pavement to keep him from hauling me back to Athena. "What about Perry?" I asked. "I ain't going anywhere till I find him." I turned my head to hide the tears running down my face. It seemed I cried as easy as a baby these days. Must be I was still weak from the fever.

Nate considered what I'd said. "The Widow Baxter's folks live here in Baltimore, just around the corner from the judge," he told me. "I know one of their house girls. Maybe Pamela's seen the boy."

He led me back the way we'd come, a long uphill climb. By the time we got to the top, I was bone weary. At last Nate came to a halt in front of a house even grander than the judge's place. Its tall glass windows sparkled in the sunlight, and its brass railings shone so bright it almost hurt my eyes to look at them. The shutters and door were painted a glossy black, and the gray stone walls looked thick enough to withstand cannon balls.

"This here is where the widow's folks live," Nate said. "Kirby's their name."

I studied the big stone house. It seemed like a fortress locked tight against me. Even if Perry was inside, I didn't see how Nate and I would get him out.

Nate tugged my sleeve. "Come on, Jesse. You want the widow to see you standing here, staring at the house?"

I came to my senses and followed Nate down a narrow alleyway between the Kirbys' house and the house next door. Soon he was knocking softly on the back door.

The slave who opened it was young and pretty. She seemed both pleased and surprised to see Nate.

"Morning, Pamela," Nate said. "You're looking mighty fine today."

"What are you doing here at this time of day?" Pamela asked, giving him a big smile to show she was teasing him. "Don't you have work to do?"

"I done it all early," he said. "Polished the judge's boots, tended to the horses, mended a busted carriage wheel."

Pamela noticed me standing behind Nate. "Who's this raggedy white boy tagging along with you?" she asked.

Nate patted my shoulder. "This here's Jesse Sherman, come all the way from Talbot County. He's seeking a little slave child named Perry. Colonel Botfield might have brought him here a few weeks back."

Pamela stared at me distrustfully, all the happiness gone from her face. "What do you want him for?"

"It ain't what you think," I said, fearing she believed I was a slave catcher after a reward. "I promised Perry's mama I'd bring him to Miss Polly Baxter, but the colonel stole him away from me. Is he here?"

Pamela glanced at Nate. He shrugged. "Athena swears Jesse's a good boy," he told her.

Pamela hesitated, still unsure, I guess. "Is Perry about seven years old?" she asked. "Blue-eyed and fair-skinned?"

I nodded. "That's him! Have you seen him?"

"Not since the night Colonel Botfield carried him

through the front door," Pamela said slowly. "I let them in. The child was putting up a mighty struggle, kicking and hitting and carrying on. A regular little hellion he was."

Worried as I was, I couldn't help smiling at the picture she was painting of Perry. It seemed the colonel hadn't busted the child's spirit any more than he'd busted the spirit of that man I'd seen in the slave jail.

"Miss Henrietta came flying to meet him," Pamela went on. "Her face was terrible to see—cold and hard and full of hate. She snatched the child out of the colonel's arms and told him she'd only give him half the reward because he didn't have the boy's mother."

"That's because she died," I put in, but Pamela went on telling her story as if I hadn't spoken.

"Before Miss Henrietta knew what he was up to, the colonel grabbed Perry back. 'The boy's a pretty thing,' he said. 'Unless you give me the whole amount, I got half a mind to keep him for myself. 'Tain't my fault his mama died.' 'You forget, Uncle,' Miss Henrietta cried. 'I own the boy! You have no right to him!'"

At this point, Nate touched Pamela's hand. "Hush," he whispered. "You want the whole household to hear you?"

Pamela looked over her shoulder, but the kitchen was empty. Taking a deep breath, she went on in a lower voice. "They stood there arguing till Mr. Kirby came downstairs to see what the trouble was. By then, Miss Henrietta looked a sight, red-faced and rageful. The boy was still kicking and hitting, biting and hollering fit to kill. Only the colonel was his usual self, smirking like Satan at the ruckus he'd caused."

Pamela paused to listen to a sound from inside the house. Satisfied no one was coming to the door, she continued her story. "Miss Henrietta told her daddy the colonel had brought her slave child back but refused to hand him over unless she paid him the whole reward, even though he didn't have the boy's mother. Then the colonel spoke up and said he had claims on both the boy and his mother. Mr. Kirby said that was all water under the bridge and that the child belonged to Henrietta."

Pamela shook her head. "I never saw such carryings-on. While the colonel swore a blue streak, Miss Henrietta walked off with the child. Mr. Kirby spied me standing there and told me to fetch a bottle of whiskey for him and the colonel. They stayed in the study drinking and playing cards for the rest of the night."

"Where is Perry now?" I peered through the doorway, hoping to see him somewhere. "Is he still here?"

"Miss Henrietta keeps him locked in a room in the cellar," Pamela said. "She won't let anyone go near him. There's no telling what that woman intends to do with the poor child."

I was ready to rescue Perry then and there, but Pamela stopped me. "Not now. Colonel Abednego Botfield has been staying here ever since he showed up with Perry. At this very minute, he's talking treason with a roomful of bankers and politicians. He's got rifles to sell to the Confederates, he says, good ones, and if they—"

A bell on the kitchen wall jangled behind her. "That's the library," she said. "The gentlemen must be wanting more brandy. You'd best leave before someone catches me talking to you."

Scared as I was of the colonel, I didn't aim to go running off without Perry. "We can't leave that boy here," I told Nate. "The widow's bound to be the death of him."

Pamela hesitated, looking fearful. "Come back after midnight," she whispered. "I'll meet you here at the door. We'll get the child out of the house somehow."

The bell jangled again, longer this time, and Pamela shooed us away. "Go on," she warned us. "Mr. Kirby will be poking his head out the library door any second now."

By the time Nate and I got back to the Baxters' house, I was so tuckered out I could scarcely put one foot in front of the other. Athena took one look at me and snapped at Nate, "You must have walked this poor boy all over Baltimore. Didn't I tell you he's still weak? You aim to kill him?"

"Now, now, don't get all het up, Athena," Nate said. "The boy's fine."

Truth to tell, I felt more dead than alive, but I done my best to hide it. I didn't want Athena putting me back to bed and dosing me with swamp water, not when Perry was in worse danger of dying than I was.

Athena turned to me. "Did you learn Perry's whereabouts?"

"The widow's got him locked in the cellar at the Kirbys' house," I said. "But Pamela's going to help Nate and me get him out of there tonight."

Athena turned to Nate, her face creased with worry. "Surely you ain't aiming to take a risk like that. What's going to happen when the Kirbys find the boy gone? And how about Pamela? You given any thought to what they might do to her?"

Nate studied the tabletop a second or two. "The child's sure to die if we don't get him out of there," he said in a low voice.

Athena turned away. "Lord help him," she whispered. "Lord help you, too, Nate."

"Didn't I tell you that there boy would bring us grief?" Nate asked, jerking his thumb at me.

Athena laid a hand on my shoulder and frowned at Nate. "You can't blame Jesse for what the colonel and the widow done."

"Huh" was all Nate said. He didn't have to say more, for I knew what he was thinking. I was a white boy from across the Bay. My uncle owned a slave and leaned strong toward the South. Worse yet, my granddaddy and my great-granddaddy and on back before them had bought and sold slaves.

"Well," Athena said with a long quivery sigh, "I reckon you're going to do what you have to do, and that's that."

Nate nodded and turned his mind to the dinner Athena set before us. Sweet potatoes and ham slices, corn muffins and turnip greens. It was a mighty fine meal, but I didn't relish it as much as I might have, for I was scared of what might happen at the Kirbys' house.

When I'd eaten all I could, Athena took my plate and told me to go down to the basement. "The judge will be coming home soon," she said. "It won't do for him to see you sitting at the table, enjoying his food."

Late that night, Nate woke me from a troubled dream. "Time to go," he said.

I followed him out the back door and down the alley. I didn't care for Baltimore in the daylight, but it was far worse at night. The moon shone down on the narrow streets, casting long black shadows. I expected Colonel Abednego Botfield to pop out from every alley we passed. He could be lurking in a dark doorway, he could be hunkering behind a wall. Like the devil himself, he could be anywhere, casting his snares, ready to pounce. By the time we reached the Kirbys' house, I was as jumpy as a grasshopper at harvest time.

As quiet as quiet can be, we sneaked around to the back door. Nate tapped softly, and Pamela opened it so fast we almost fell into the kitchen.

"Colonel Botfield and Mr. Kirby are still in the library," she whispered, "drinking and playing cards. I think the colonel's fixing to win every cent Mr. Kirby owns. I heard him joking about winning the boy."

That was bad news. But there was no going back now. We had to get Perry out of that house before the colonel got his hands on him again.

Pamela took a key ring from a hook by the cellar door and lit a small candle. We followed her down a creaky flight of steps into a dark, narrow hall. The ceiling was so low Nate had to stoop to keep from hitting his head. The cold, damp air smelled as old as the earth. The place was a sight worse than the judge's cellar, that's for sure.

I started to say something, but Pamela motioned to a row of closed doors. I could hear someone snoring and someone else coughing. A bed creaked. A voice muttered.

"Don't wake the others," Pamela whispered. "No one must know I had anything to do with the boy's disappearance."

At the end of the hall we came to a locked door. Pamela tried several keys before she found one that fit. Stepping over the threshold, she held the candle high. Rats squeaked and scurried away from its light, making the straw on the floor rustle. In one corner, curled into a motionless ball, was Perry.

Fearing he was dead, I dropped to my knees beside him and whispered his name.

He sat up and backed away, hands raised to shield his face. "Don't," he cried, "don't!"

I reached for him. "Hush, Perry. It's me, Jesse. Nobody's going to hurt you."

Slowly his eyes focused on me. To my surprise, he flung his arms around me. "Jesse," he cried. "Where have you been all this time? I thought you'd gone back home and I'd never see you again. I thought you—"

"I came as soon as I could," I cut in, "but my head was busted and I was sick of a fever and I—"

Nate pushed me aside gently and lifted Perry from the filthy straw. With Pamela and me following close on his heels, he carried the child from his prison.

My heart was pounding so loud I thought the colonel might hear it and come to investigate. He wouldn't hit me with the butt of his revolver this time. No, sir. He'd shoot me, kill me for sure. And Perry and Nate, too, most likely.

In the kitchen, Pamela blew out the candle and quietly opened the back door. "Go quick," she whispered.

Down the hall behind us, I heard the colonel laughing. "Looks like I win again, Daniel!"

As Mr. Kirby bellowed a string of cuss words, I eased outside on shaking legs. Any minute those two would come looking for brandy and see us.

Eager as I was to go, I waited while Nate hesitated on the doorstep. "Come with us, Pamela," he said. "You're bound to be blamed for this."

She shook her head. "I'll get in more trouble running away."

Nate seized her arm. "Listen to me," he begged. "I got it all thought out. We'll go to the Yankee camp on Federal Hill. I hear they shelter runaways as long as we do a good day's work for them."

But Pamela didn't budge. "You go," she said. "Join

up with the Yankees and do their dirty work, but don't expect me to come along with you."

The bell on the kitchen wall jangled, but Pamela was too busy arguing with Nate to pay it any mind. I plucked at his arm. "Come on," I whispered. "They're wanting more to drink."

A door opened somewhere, and I heard the colonel say, "That worthless wench of yours must be asleep. Am I going to have to get the brandy myself?"

Perry tightened his grip on Nate and began to whimper. "He's coming, he's coming. I hear him!"

"Please go, Nate," Pamela begged, but it was too late. Just as she started to close the door, a red-faced man stepped into the kitchen.

"Didn't you hear me ringing the bell, girl?" he hollered. "Where's my brandy?"

"I'm sorry, Mr. Kirby. Go sit down, sir, I'll bring it to you." Pamela tried to block his view, but, drunk as he was, the man managed to spot Nate.

"Who's at the door?" he asked, peering around Pamela. "You entertaining callers, girl?"

Nate thrust Perry at me. "Get him out of here!"

At the same moment, I glimpsed Colonel Abednego Botfield following his host into the kitchen. Terrified, I staggered backward into the alley, hauling Perry into the shadows with me.

I heard Nate say, "Sorry, sir, but I been drinking with my friends and I got the notion to see Pamela. She told me to go away, so I guess I best leave now." He was slurring his voice and putting on a good show, but Mr. Kirby wasn't done with him yet.

"Does Judge Baxter know you're out so late?" he asked. "If you was my slave, you wouldn't be traipsing around the streets at this hour. The judge gives you way too much freedom."

Colonel Botfield stepped forward. "Is someone with you?" he asked Nate.

"No, sir, it's just me."

"I thought I heard a noise in the alley," the colonel said. "Excuse me while I take a look."

I started running then, faster than I thought possible, dragging Perry along with me. Behind me I heard the colonel shout, "Stop right there or I'll shoot!"

His gun went off, but the bullet went wide. I heard it hit the wall over my head as I ducked around the corner. On St. Paul Street, the two of us tumbled down a flight of steps and crouched in the shadows by a basement door. Scarcely breathing, we heard Colonel Botfield pounding up the alley toward us.

He stopped at the corner, breathing hard like he wasn't used to running. I pictured him sniffing the air like a hound seeking our scent. It wouldn't have surprised me none if the man had dropped to all fours and followed our trail with his nose.

"Abednego," Mr. Kirby called. "Come on back here. We ain't finished our card game. I aim to win back every cent I lost, you old rascal."

The Colonel hawked a gob of something nasty into

the gutter. "Don't let that Negro go," he hollered. "Him and that gal of yours are up to something, and I mean to learn what it is."

Letting fly a stream of curses, he strode down the alley, his boot heels clicking against the stones.

"He didn't see us, did he?" Perry whispered.

I let out my breath in a long sigh. "That man don't miss much, but if he'd seen us, we'd be dead now, shot through the head."

We waited a while longer just in case the colonel was lurking somewhere close by. A church bell struck the half hour and then the quarter hour. I tiptoed to the top of the steps. Didn't see nothing but a pitiful three-legged dog limping down the empty street.

"Let's go," I said. "The Baxters' house ain't far from here."

"Does Polly know I'm coming?" Perry asked, close to tears by now. "Is she waiting there for me?"

I hated to tell the poor child bad news when he was already feeling low, but it made no sense to get his hopes up. "Polly's daddy sent her and her mother to his brother's place in the country. I never got a chance to tell her nothing about you."

Perry sniffed hard and wiped his eyes, but he didn't say a thing, just tottered along beside me, weak as a baby. For a little child, he had a lot of pluck.

"I hear you put up a real good fight when the colonel brought you to the Kirbys' house," I said.

Perry shuddered. "The widow just about whipped

every bit of fight out of me," he said. "All that kept me from dying was Mama."

I looked at him. The moonlight silvered his face but not his eyes, giving him a ghostly look. "What do you mean, Perry?"

"Mama was there with me," he said in a dreamy voice, "deep in the shadows, where no one could see her but me. She told me you'd come for me. I didn't believe her, but she was right."

"You must have had a fever dream," I told him. "I've had some that seemed realer than real life."

"No," he said. "Mama was there. She was so close I felt her dress brush against my face."

It fair gave me the shivers to hear the child talk so. I glanced over my shoulder, half expecting to see Lydia watching us from an alleyway. But there was no sign of her. No sign of the colonel or Nate either. I urged Perry to walk faster. Never had a night seemed so dark and full of danger.

When we got to Baxters' house, Athena met us at the kitchen door. "Oh, sweet Lord!" she cried, hugging Perry tight. "What has that woman done to you?"

Now that I could see Perry better, I realized he'd been badly treated indeed. He was cut and bruised, and his clothes were nothing but filthy rags. From the looks of him, it seemed the widow had planned to keep the child locked up till he died of starvation. Or a beating or something even worse.

With me following close behind, Athena carried

Perry downstairs and laid him on my pallet. I watched her bathe his face the way she'd once bathed mine, fussing over him like a mother hen. When she'd done what she could, she straightened up and looked at me.

"Why didn't Nate carry this poor child here instead of making him walk?" she asked, clearly vexed. "Where is that no-'count man anyhow?"

"Mr. Kirby and Colonel Botfield have him," I said. "The colonel suspects him and Pamela are up to something, and he aims to learn what."

Athena shook her head. "That don't sound good. They're bound to come here looking for this child." She studied Perry's face a moment. "Easy to tell who his daddy was," she said softly. "I knew Peregrine when he was this boy's age and never have I seen a closer likeness."

The words were no sooner out of her mouth than we heard a loud knocking at the front door.

"Judge Baxter," an all too familiar voice hollered. "Open up. We have your slave here!"

Perry's eyes widened in fear, but Athena picked him up. "Don't worry, I'll hide you somewhere safe." Turning to me, she added, "Get out the back door fast. It sounds like the judge is letting them in."

CHAPTER 11

I scooted up those stairs like a scared rabbit, but I wasn't quick enough. At the very moment I reached the back door, Mr. Kirby and Colonel Abednego Botfield came storming down the hall toward me, followed by Judge Baxter. The colonel was dragging Nate, whose head was bleeding like he'd been beaten bad. Pistol-whipped, maybe. It made me ache to see him looking more dead than alive.

"Fetch that wench of yours," Colonel Botfield was hollering at Judge Baxter. "She's got that slave child hid in this house, I tell you."

When the colonel saw me struggling to unbolt the back door, he dropped Nate to the floor with a thud. Grabbing my shirt, he lifted me clean off my feet and shook me like a feather pillow.

"This is the very brat that hid the woman and her boy from me in Talbot County," he yelled.

Judge Baxter looked from Colonel Botfield to me and back to Colonel Botfield again. "I've never seen that guttersnipe before," he said, clearly astonished. "I have no idea why he's in my house or where he came from."

"If Jesse Sherman is here, the child I'm seeking is here, too." Colonel Botfield gave me a few more shakes hard enough to break a chicken's neck. "Give me a Bible, and I'll swear on the Holy Evangels of Almighty God that this here rascal and your no-account slave broke into Mr. Daniel Kirby's house tonight and stole a child that belongs to your son's widow."

Flummoxed, Judge Baxter stared at Colonel Botfield. I noticed he made no move to fetch a Bible. "You must be mad or drunk to say such a thing. Why in heaven's name would Nate steal a slave and bring him here?"

Growing more wrathy every second, the colonel shook me again, causing me to bite my tongue something awful. "Just give me permission to search the house," he said. "You'll soon see I'm telling the truth."

Judge Baxter drew himself up tall and straight, shoulders back and chin up. "No one searches my house, Colonel Botfield, least of all a scoundrel such as yourself."

Ignoring the insult, the colonel said, "As I've already told you, the slave in question belongs to the widow of your deceased son! I should think you'd want to help the bereaved reclaim her property."

Instead of shaking me again, Colonel Botfield commenced to twist my collar as if he meant to choke me to death.

Judge Baxter looked at me. "Loosen your grip on the boy," he said slowly to the colonel, "before you kill him."

Colonel Botfield let me go with a box on the ears that made my head ring like a church bell. "Will you or won't you give me permission to search the house?"

"In the name of God, Horatio," put in Mr. Kirby, "let the colonel do as he asks. Ain't you and me friends as well as in-laws?"

"It's not you I object to, Daniel. It's the company you keep." The judge eyed the colonel with contempt. "That man may be your wife's brother, but he's no gentleman. Furthermore, I don't appreciate him telling me what to do in my own house. Nor do I appreciate the way he's beaten my slave."

Just then Athena came upstairs, doing her best to look puzzled by the commotion. She drew in her breath at the sight of Nate lying on the floor, but she didn't say a word.

Judge Baxter frowned at Athena. "My son's widow is apparently missing a slave child. Do you know his whereabouts?"

Athena looked at the floor. Instead of speaking up the way I expected her to, she just shook her head. "No, sir," she whispered. "I don't know nothing about it, sir."

"How about this boy?" The colonel grabbed me and gave me another teeth-rattling shake. "What the devil is Jesse Sherman doing here?"

Athena's face softened. Turning to the judge, she said, "Oh, sir, that poor child showed up this evening, begging at the back door. I fed him a few scraps and let him shelter by the fire. I didn't think you'd mind, sir."

The colonel cursed. "That's a damnable lie. I left the rascal for dead in the street at least three weeks ago. You been caring for him all this while, aiding and abetting him to steal the widow's slave child."

"Please let us search this house, Horatio," Mr. Kirby put in. "Henrietta is beside herself, she loves the child so."

I wanted to call the man a liar, but, if I spoke up, they'd all know I'd seen Perry. So, like Athena, I kept my mouth shut.

The judge sighed heavily and headed for the cellar door. "Come with me," he said to the men. "You'll soon see I have nothing to hide."

The moment the judge's back was turned, Colonel Botfield grabbed my arm and twisted it pretty near out of the socket. "No matter how this little scene plays out," he whispered, "you ain't seen the last of me, Jesse Sherman. As sure as the sun rises in the east and sets in the west, I'll be your death, boy."

I broke away, my nose full of the brimstone smell of his smoky breath, and moved closer to Athena. Shaking with fear, she put her arm around me.

"Come along, Abednego," Mr. Kirby called from the cellar door. "Forget the boy for now."

But Colonel Botfield caught hold of me again and

dragged me down the stairs behind him. "I ain't letting the scalawag out of my sight," he said.

Those three men searched the cellar from one end to the other, peering into every corner, poking and prodding, but they found nothing. It seemed Athena had spirited Perry away. Or conjured him right out of his shape. Delia had told me tales of a witch woman down in the marsh who had the power to change people into frogs or mice or whatever she chose. Maybe Athena had the same magical arts, for there wasn't a sign of Perry anywhere. I glimpsed a mouse in the corner, though, watching us with bright eyes.

At last Judge Baxter turned to Colonel Botfield. "I hope you're satisfied," he said. "Didn't I tell you the child was not in my house?"

"No, I ain't satisfied. That wench of yours has got him hid in some hidey hole only she knows about." The wily old scoundrel scowled at me and added, "This boy knows more than he's telling. If you was to hand him over to me for a few hours, I'd get the truth out of him fast enough."

To my relief, Judge Baxter shook his head. "In your hands, there's no telling what would become of him," he told the colonel. "If the boy aided and abetted, I'll see he goes to court, where he'll receive a fair trial."

"At least promise me this," the colonel said. "Lock him up and keep him till we get to the bottom of the affair. Him and your slave both."

Judge Baxter merely shrugged and said he'd consider it. "And now, gentlemen," he concluded, "if you'll excuse me, I wish to go to bed. I have a full schedule at the courthouse tomorrow."

With that, the judge led Mr. Kirby and Colonel Botfield to the back door and opened it as if he was letting out a pair of no-'count hounds. To Mr. Kirby, he said, "Daniel, our friendship will be sorely tested if you bring your brother-in-law to my house again."

After the door slammed shut behind the two, Judge Baxter bent over Nate. Athena had wiped the blood from his face and was bandaging his head. I was glad to see Nate's eyes were open but sorry to see the damage the colonel had done to him.

"I don't know who or what to believe," the judge said to Nate, "but as much as I hate to agree with Abednego Botfield, I smell the rank odor of mendacity."

Fearing the judge would lay all the blame on Nate, I thrust myself between them. "It ain't Nate's fault," I said. "He was just helping me, sir. I'm the one who stole Perry and you should be glad I did, for he's your own kin—"

That got the judge's attention all right. Towering over me as wrathy as one of them kings in the Bible, he roared, "My kin? What do you mean by that?"

Too late I recalled what Athena had told me about saying such things, but there was no taking the words back now. "Perry's daddy was the late Peregrine Baxter," I hollered, too wrathy myself to care what the man did to me. "That makes Perry your grandson. Your own flesh and blood."

Whilst I was talking, the judge was hauling me to the door. "Liar," he roared. "My son would never miscegenate with a slave!"

"If you saw him," I yelled back, "you'd know I'm telling the truth!"

The judge was so mad I doubt he heard a word I said, let alone believed me. With one last curse, he threw me out the door like I was no more than a bundle of rags.

I hit the ground so hard it knocked the wind right out of me. For a second I thought I was dead or paralyzed, but then I got my breath and picked myself up. The door was shut fast, but the kitchen window showed the lamp was still lit. I sneaked up and looked inside. The judge was talking to Nate, his face grim. Athena hovered nearby, wringing her hands with worry. There was nothing I could do but wait till the judge went to bed. Then, if I was lucky, Athena might let me in and tell me where Perry was.

It seemed like a long time, probably because I was cold and tired and wanted nothing more than a warm place to sleep, but at last the kitchen door opened and Athena peeked out. "Jesse?" she whispered.

I scurried into the house. "Where's Nate?" I whispered.

"The judge sent him to the cellar and told me not to go near him," Athena said. "He's mighty angry at both of us."

"And Perry? Where's he?"

"Come on," Athena said, "I'll show you."

I followed her down to a small storage room in the cellar where she put me to work moving a stack of barrels and crates. I recalled the judge poking around in the same place, but he'd contented himself with shining his lantern here and there. I guess Athena knew more about the cellar than he did, for the barrels and crates hid a tiny room the judge had missed altogether.

Inside was Perry, curled up in a blanket, sound asleep and as safe as a mole in the ground. I grinned a big grin, mightily relieved to see him.

"Crawl in there with him and get some sleep, Jesse," Athena said. "I'll fetch you in the morning after the judge has gone to the courthouse."

As quiet as I could, I wriggled under Perry's blanket, bone weary and glad for the warmth of his body. I thought I'd tumble into sleep the minute I shut my eyes, but long after Athena moved the crates back into place, I lay awake worrying. Even though I'd saved Perry from the widow, I was far from done with him. Grandson or not, the judge didn't want any part of the boy. It seemed we had no choice but to travel on and find Miss Polly.

When I finally managed to fall asleep, I dreamed I was sailing down the Bay toward home. The sky was blue and the water sparkled. I could see Uncle Philemon waiting on shore for me, waving to beat the band. My heart leaped with joy, but before the boat docked, the sky turned black and the wind commenced to blow. Uncle Philemon disappeared. Captain Harrison turned to tell me something, but he had Colonel Abednego Botfield's face. In his hand was a pistol, pointed at my head.

That was when I woke up to see Nate bending over me. One eye was swollen shut and his cheek was bruised, the colonel's handiwork. "Athena send me to fetch you boys," he said. "The judge has left for the day, and we got plans to make."

Nate woke Perry next. For a second the poor child's eyes widened in fear, but Nate told him not to worry. "You're safe now. That woman won't never get her hands on you again."

Athena met us at the top of the stairs. She'd fixed oatmeal for all three of us and a mug of steaming hot coffee for Nate and me.

Perry looked around the room wildly. "Are we safe here?" he asked. "What if somebody sees us through the window? What if the colonel comes back?"

Athena drew Perry on to her lap and rocked him. "Bless you, child, nobody's coming into the backyard to peek through that little old kitchen window. Company knocks at the front door. You're as safe as bird in its nest here."

Gently she scooped up a spoonful of oatmeal and offered it to him. "You eat this," she said. "You need to put some meat on those skinny bones and get strong."

While we ate, Athena asked if we'd slept all right, were we warm enough, how did we feel, did we want more to eat, and so on. She felt Perry's forehead to see if he was feverish, she changed the bandage on Nate's head, she inspected his swollen eye, she forced me take another dose of the foul concoction she'd made for me while I was sick. Truth to tell, I believe we enjoyed being fussed over, even Nate.

The only thing I took exception to was the scrubbing she gave Perry and me. Much as I hated soap and water, it was good to put on clean clothes afterwards. Peregrine's castoffs, Athena said, still packed away in a trunk upstairs. My pants were a little short and Perry's were a little long, but on the whole we looked a sight more respectable than before.

When Athena had done what she could, she studied all three of us, sighed real heavy, and turned to Nate. "I know you're going to take your chances with the Yankee army, but what about Pamela? She must be in bad trouble with the Kirbys. You just going to leave her to face it alone?"

Nate shook his head. "I aim to get her out of that house one way or another. And the sooner the better. I don't think I'll have no trouble persuading her to come with me now."

Athena gave me a long look. "Jesse, are you still aiming to take this child to Miss Polly?"

"I promised his mama," I said once again. "I swore on her very grave."

Athena laid a piece of paper on the table. "I drew you a map. Look at it real hard. Make sure you know what you're getting into."

I studied Athena's handiwork, turning the paper

this way and that, but I couldn't make no sense of it. Finally I said, "There must be some mistake. Surely you don't mean us to cross the Potomac River. Why, if we do that, we'll be in Virginia. That's south."

"If you want to see Miss Polly Baxter," Athena said, "Virginia's exactly where you have to go."

I opened my mouth to protest, but Athena hadn't finished what she was saying. Turning to Perry, she added, "You got more kin than Miss Polly, you know. Your mama's sister Hyacinth is in Virginia, too. The judge sent her to his brother's place to look after Miss Polly and Mrs. Baxter."

Perry stared at Athena, just as surprised as I was. "Mama never told me she had a sister," he said.

"You have a granny, too," Athena said. "Did your mama ever speak of her?"

Perry shook his head, still not believing. "I have a grandmother? Why didn't Mama send me to her?"

"She's a slave like you and your Aunt Hyacinth," Athena said quietly. "How could she help you?"

Perry didn't have an answer for that. But I was full of wonderment. Once I'd thought the poor child was all alone in the world. Now it seemed he had more kin than I did, both white and black.

"Is my grandmother in Virginia, too?" Perry asked. "I'd dearly love to meet her."

"Mr. Peregrine sold your granny south about eight or nine years ago," Athena said, "around the same time he sent Hyacinth here." She glanced at Nate, but he just sat there drinking his coffee as if all this had nothing to do with him.

"The last I heard your granny was on a plantation not far from where you're going," Athena went on. "But I believe there's a good chance she and Hyacinth—"

Nate got Athena's attention by slamming down his coffee cup. Scowling something fierce, he shook his head at her. It was clear a secret hung in the air between them, a secret Nate wanted kept from Perry and me.

Perry looked from one to the other, his face full of puzzlement. Like me, he wanted to ask more questions, but it was useless. Neither Nate nor Athena was about to say another word on the subject.

"Now, Jesse, about this map." Athena tapped my hand to get my attention. "You take the train from Camden Street Station to New Berlin and cross the Potomac on the ferry there. Mr. Cornelius Baxter's place is called Waterside. You can't see it from the river, too many trees. Just take the first road you come to and follow it to the top of the hill. Big brick house. Can't miss it."

She paused, and I studied the sketch she'd made, working hard to memorize the names of the places I had to go. I knew my letters, but sometimes it was hard to figure out the words they made. As Uncle Philemon often remarked, I was an ignorant boy and like to stay that way, and what did it matter as long as I knew how to hammer and saw.

"The house ain't hard to find," Nate put in. "Both

113

Athena and me have gone there with the judge's family."

"How far is it?" I asked.

"Oh, forty, fifty miles," he said. "You'll be on the train most of the way."

"But what if somebody wants to know what I'm doing with a little slave boy?" I asked, ever the one to worry.

Perry gave me a dirty look, but Nate just shrugged. "Ain't nobody paying any heed to children these days," he said. "They got more important things to worry about what with the war coming and soldiers everywhere."

Athena nodded. "You won't have no trouble, Jesse, as long as you don't do anything to attract notice." She went to the fireplace, reached into a bowl on the mantel, and pulled out a handful of silver coins. "Use some of the grocery money for your train tickets," she said. "The judge will never miss it. Should be enough for the ferry as well."

I thanked her and pocketed the money. Nate rose to his feet. "Let's go before someone comes knocking on the door."

Athena hugged Perry. "Nate's right. Linger too long and the colonel might show up again."

"Ain't you coming with us?" I asked. "The judge is bound to be mad as the very devil when he finds out Nate's gone."

"Don't you worry about me, Jesse." Athena drew

herself up tall and folded her arms across her chest. "The judge won't do nothing. He needs me to take care of him."

She opened the door and let in the morning smell of wood smoke and city dirt. "Just promise me one thing," she said. "Find Hyacinth as soon as you get there. Don't talk to nobody till you talk to her. The judge sends Polly down there every summer for the fresh air and Hyacinth always goes along to wait on her. She knows all there is to know about that family. Knows the lay of the land, too." Athena chuckled. "Why, Hyacinth's even got her own cabin she's down there so much."

"Come on now, Athena," Nate said softly. "I know you hate to see these children leave, but I got to get going whilst I can."

Without giving me a chance to do more than call good-bye to Athena, Nate hustled Perry and me down the alley to Centre Street. I expected to see the colonel come around every corner, but for once there was no sign of the old devil. Even so, I was sure I hadn't seen the last of him. Somewhere, sometime we were bound to meet again. I only hoped I'd be ready for him.

CHAPTER 12

Near Pratt Street, Nate ducked into an alley. We were so close to the docks, I could smell the Bay. All of a sudden, I was so homesick I could scarcely keep myself from running off to search for Captain Harrison. If only I could go sailing home to Uncle Philemon. Let the old codger skin my hide. I'd thank him for it. What's more, I'd bring him all the turtles in the marsh. A bushel of crabs, a bucket of oysters, a string of bluefish, a muskrat—whatever his heart desired I'd get and never say a word of complaint.

I glanced at Nate. If I was to scarper right this second, he wouldn't dare chase me through the streets of Baltimore. What's more, I could leave Perry with him. Nate could take the child to the army camp, say he was his son or something. Surely the Yankees would have room for a boy as small as Perry.

But the trouble was, Nate hadn't made no promise

to Lydia, had he? I was the one who done that. So I stayed where I was, bound by a dead woman to keep my word.

Nate hugged Perry, but he shook my hand as if I was a man like him. "You be careful, Jesse. The colonel's bound to be on the lookout for you and that child."

"You be careful, too, Nate," I said, ashamed of the evil thoughts I'd been entertaining. "And don't be too trustful of those Yankees. You never know what them characters are up to."

After a few more farewells and warnings, we parted ways. Left alone with Perry, I took his arm to hurry him along. I half expected him to pull away, but he trudged beside me, saying nary a word.

The Camden Street Station was mobbed with folks. Seemed like half the city of Baltimore was leaving for someplace else. To add to the crying babies and pushing crowds, Federal soldiers marched here and there, following orders shouted by officers. Some folks jeered the soldiers, but most were too busy with their own affairs to pay them or anyone else any attention.

I was glad of the crowd, for it made it easy to buy our train tickets without attracting undue notice. The man took my coins without so much as looking at me. "Next train leaves in five minutes," he said and turned to the customer waiting behind me.

Perry and I boarded the train with a large crowd of soldiers. I figured a bunch of Federals would have no interest in a couple of boys. Like Nate said, they'd have other things on their minds. Keeping the rebels from blowing up the railroad, for instance.

Before the train even left the station, some of the soldiers had their cards out. One played a mouth organ. Another had a banjo. They were full of high spirits, laughing and joking and smoking the vilest cigars I ever smelled.

The whistle blew, the cars lurched, and soon we were moving. Perry slumped lower in his seat and pressed his face against the window, but this was my first train ride and I aimed to enjoy it. So I joined in the jollity and sang "Old Dan Tucker," "Camptown Races," and "Buffalo Gals" along with the soldiers. It didn't matter if I knew all the words or not. I just hollered away.

Once we passed over a high bridge way above the treetops. Truth to tell, it scared me a little to look down. I'd never been up so high in my whole life. I heard someone say it was the Thomas Viaduct, a great feat of engineering and famous throughout the country, but I couldn't help worrying the train might jump the tracks and we'd all go plummeting down to certain death and dismemberment. I reckon that was my view of the world. If something could go wrong, it would, and most likely I'd be there when it happened.

At the Relay depot, I saw Federal soldiers swaggering around like they owned the place. I guessed they were on guard duty, but they were having a good time anyway, lolling in the sun and waving to us as we passed by. It seemed to me they led an easy life with nothing much to do.

A soldier in the seat across the aisle from me leaned over and asked where I was bound. He was a short, skinny fellow, not much older than me, but he was sporting a wispy little mustache.

"New Berlin," I told him, hoping he wouldn't ask no questions about Perry.

He whistled. "You'll see a fair amount of activity there. Rebels everywhere, I hear. Causing all sorts of mischief, too. Burning bridges and stopping trains and I don't know what all."

"Is that right?" My heart beat a little faster at the thought of seeing some actual warfare.

The young man nodded. "My name's Otis Hicks," he said by way of introducing himself. "Private Otis Hicks, Pennsylvania Infantry."

I told him my name and where I was from. "Not meaning to be disrespectful or nothing," I went on, "but you look mighty young to be in the army."

"I'm only fifteen," he confessed, "but I told the men at the recruiting station I was eighteen. Stood on my tiptoes when they measured me. I sure fooled them."

With some envy I studied the shiny brass buttons on his jacket. "You reckon I could pass for eighteen?" I asked.

Otis grinned and shook his head. "Maybe next year, if you stretch yourself as much as you can. And manage to grow one of these." He touched that fuzz on his lip like it was something to be proud of. "Why do you want to be a soldier?"

"Same reason you do, I reckon. Win fame and glory and such."

Otis nodded. "I can't hardly wait for the fighting to start. I aim to kill me at least one rebel a day."

"What if you get killed instead?"

He fingered his mustache again like it was cat that might purr if he petted it long enough. "Me? I'm too smart to catch a bullet." He laughed, but I think he really believed what he'd said.

"I sure hope you're right, Otis," the man next to him said, but he winked at me as he spoke.

Then the two of them started talking about the war and what they'd do when they finally got a chance to fight the rebels. To hear them talk, the Confederates might as well surrender right now and save everybody a passel of trouble.

While the two of them tried to outmatch each other with boasts and brags, I glanced at Perry. Despite all the racket in the coach, he'd fallen fast asleep. Though I wanted to stay awake for fear of missing something, I couldn't keep my eyes open either. Voices rose and fell, the train chug-chug-chugged, swaying and bouncing over the tracks, and soon it rocked me to sleep.

The next thing I knew Private Otis Hicks was shaking me. "I'm getting off here," he said. "New Berlin's the next stop. Better keep those eyes open or you'll end up with the rebels in Harpers Ferry."

Perry woke up, and the two of us peered out the window. We were at Point of Rocks, and all the soldiers was piling off the train, shouting and laughing. I caught a glimpse of Otis and his companion and hollered, "Good luck to you in the war, Otis!" But he didn't look back. I guess he couldn't be bothered with a boy like me, not with so many important events to occupy his mind.

The train picked up speed again and we were on our way, steaming along beside what I thought was the Potomac River. Later I heard someone say it was the Chesapeake and Ohio Canal. The river itself was on the other side of the canal.

Before long the train stopped at New Berlin. Perry and I jumped to the platform, crossed the canal, and headed for the ferry along with a bunch of other folks.

The Potomac River was wide, and its water had a clean, fresh smell, different from the Bay's rich stink of salt and marsh and mud. Downstream, it ran fast between groups of rocks, swirling and foaming in the prettiest way, but upstream, it was calm. To the west, I saw hills higher than any on the Eastern Shore and mountains beyond them, the first I'd ever seen, dark against the setting sun. I could scarcely believe I was standing here, so far from home, seeing such sights. Me, Jesse Sherman, who up till recently had never been anywhere but Easton.

I made out the ferry crossing the river from the Virginia side. It wasn't much more than a big raft, towed by a cable that stretched from bank to bank.

Among the passengers were a few men and women and a couple of children. Horses and wagons, a pair of oxen, and three or four cows took up most of the space.

One of the cows mooed, and the wind carried the sound to me over the water. It made me homesick to hear it. I couldn't help wondering if I'd ever see Uncle Philemon again. What if he took sick and died before I came back? I hadn't thought I'd miss the old man, but there I stood, waiting for the ferry with tears pricking my eyes.

"It's coming, Jesse." Perry tugged at my sleeve. "See it?"

We watched the ferry get closer and closer. Soon it was nudging up against the bank, and folks began coming ashore. The man herding the cows had some trouble. Those critters made quite a commotion, bawling and carrying on, but he finally managed to get them off the ferry and onto the bank.

Then we paid our money and boarded. Once again nobody looked close at us. They was all caught up in their own affairs, talking about a skirmish between the Federals and the Confederates down the river a ways. Nobody killed, but several wounded.

"I tell you, this war ain't ever going to get going," one man opined to his companion. "Why, all they've done is fire a few shots here and there. Not one battle worth noting."

"That's the truth, Ebenezer," the other said. "The whole business ought to be settled before winter."

"Damn lot of foolishness," another said. "Tearing up railroad tracks and burning bridges is all them rebs know how to do. Can't go anywhere these days without delays."

"Why, those boys are just protecting us from Lincoln's men," the first man said. "Ain't that worth a little inconvenience, Mr. Farraday?"

"Sounds to me like we got a Union man amongst us," said Ebenezer, his face red and wrathy.

"No, boys, you misunderstood," Mr. Farraday said in a weak sort of way. "I merely meant I wish our boys would chase the Yankees back North and let us get on with our business, that's all."

The men mumbled and grumbled and kept arguing amongst themselves. Fearing things might get ugly, Perry and I moved away from them and stood by the rail. We were doing our best to avoid notice, something that hadn't overly concerned me on the train. But now that we were about to set foot in Virginia, one of the Confederate States of America, things were different. To all intents and purposes, as Uncle Philemon used to say, a foreign country lay ahead, one that had no liking for runaway slaves and those that abetted them. There was no telling what they'd think about Perry and me, and I didn't want to find out.

While we stood there acting invisible, three people joined us—a woman and a young lady, both dressed in black, accompanied by a well-dressed man.

The ladies didn't know me, but having seen them

once before, I recognized Mrs. Baxter and her daughter Polly, still dressed in mourning for the late Mr. Peregrine Baxter, deceased. Polly's face was so sweet and kind I knew Lydia had been right. She would surely welcome Perry as her nephew—which meant I'd soon be free to go home to my poor old uncle.

I figured the man with Polly and her mother to be the judge's brother, Mr. Cornelius Baxter. He was tall and stout and haughty in the way he held himself. A true southerner, I thought. Not the sort to think well of a runaway slave boy's claim to kinship. But surely Polly could win him over. And her daddy and mama, too. She would have some talking to do, I reckoned.

I moved a little closer, hoping to hear what they were saying, but Mr. Baxter gave me a look that clearly told me to move away. Nonetheless I managed to pick up a word here and there. It seemed they'd been to Frederick City to shop for dress fabric. Polly had been distressed by the sight of Yankee soldiers loitering everywhere, blocking the sidewalk, spitting tobacco, and using bad language.

"I'll be so happy to be back in Virginia," Polly said, her voice rising as if she wanted to be sure everyone around her knew where her loyalties lay. "I won't cross this river again till those ill-bred Yankees have gone back where they came from."

"If the judge had any sense, he'd join us here for the duration," Mrs. Baxter said. "I hear Baltimore is totally overrun with Lincoln's men. I fear for Horatio's safety."

Mr. Cornelius Baxter muttered something I couldn't hear. Polly turned her attention to the sunset, and her mother went on conversing softly with Mr. Baxter. "Had my son Peregrine lived," she said, "he would most certainly have gone to Richmond with his cousins."

Mr. Baxter nodded in agreement. "Peregrine would have made a fine officer."

At that point, the ferry reached the bank. With Perry and me at their heels, the Baxters strode ashore. They never once looked at us and so had no idea their own kin was following behind them. If I hadn't been so edgy, I might have laughed out loud. As it was, I watched them get into a waiting carriage and rattle off into the dusk.

As soon as they were out of sight, Perry and I trudged up the same road the carriage had taken. Even though it was late May, the evening air was cold. I would have given a lot for a nice warm jacket.

"Did you notice the pretty young lady on the ferry?" I asked Perry.

"The one dressed in black?"

I nodded. "Well, she just happens to be your aunt, Miss Polly Baxter herself!" I grinned at him. "What do you think of that?"

"She was pretty," he said in a low voice.

"Why, she's the most beautiful young lady I ever did see!" I gave him a poke. "Ain't you the lucky one?"

"Did you hear what she was saying about those Yankee soldiers in Frederick City?" he asked.

"Oh, that was just talk. She didn't mean nothing by it except she was vexed," I said, trying to pump him up as well as myself. "Just wait till she hears whose child you are. She'll love you to death."

But the stubborn boy just sighed and plodded along beside me, kicking stones as he went. Try as hard as I might, I couldn't coax another word out of him. I never did see a child who could clam up tighter than that little rascal.

At last we came to the top of a hill. By then it was pretty near dark. The Baxter place was straight ahead, set well back on a grassy lawn. Light shone from its windows and smoke curled out of the chimneys, scenting the air with the cozy smell of supper cooking.

Fearful of rousing dogs, we made a wide swing around the house and stole up through the woods to a row of small cabins. The doors were shut tight, but I chose one and rapped softly. Perry stood beside me, close enough for me to feel him shivering in the cold.

The door opened a crack, and a woman peered out at me. "Who are you? What do you want?" she asked in a low voice. I couldn't blame her for being suspicious. The last thing she'd expected to see was a pair of strangers standing on her doorstep.

"We've come all the way from Baltimore City looking for a slave woman named Hyacinth," I whispered. "Athena, the Baxters' house woman, sent us."

The woman pointed down the row. "Hyacinth lives in the last cabin, but I reckon she's still at the big house, tending to Miss Polly. Just set on the steps and wait. She'll be along shortly." With that she closed the door.

Perry and I did what she said, but it was sheer torment to sit there smelling dinner cooking for everyone but us. Behind the closed doors of the cabins, we heard folks talking and laughing. I pictured them eating and drinking, filling their bellies whilst Perry and me huddled together in the dark, cold, scared, and hungry.

Somewhere hounds bayed. Across the river, a train whistle blew sad and low. Never had I felt so lonesome in my whole life.

"We shouldn't have come here," Perry whispered.

"Seems to me we didn't have much choice," I reminded him. "We couldn't very well stay in Talbot County or Baltimore, could we? Not with the colonel and the widow on our tails."

As usual, he didn't have nothing more to say. He sat there hunched in misery like a baby bird waiting to be fed.

At last I saw someone walking toward us from the big house. Even in the dark, I noticed she had nervous way of holding herself, like she was pondering a weighty problem. I knew she wouldn't see us till she fell over us, so I got to my feet and pulled Perry up beside me.

"Hey," I called softly. "Is your name Hyacinth?"

Although I'd hoped not to startle her, she went as tense as a deer that just got a whiff of danger. Stopping where she was, she peered at Perry and me. "Who wants to know?" she whispered.

"I'm Jesse Sherman from Talbot County," I told her. "I got your sister Lydia's boy, Perry, with me."

"Lydia?" Hyacinth came toward us, still wary. "You know Lydia?"

Perry broke away from me and ran to meet Hyacinth. "Mama's dead," he blurted out. "Mama's dead. And so is Papa."

Hyacinth studied his tearful face a second and then drew him close. Perry clung to her as if he never meant to let go, sobbing fit to bust. Hyacinth began to cry, too.

For a long while neither Perry nor Hyacinth paid me any mind. Not that I expected them to. But I couldn't help wishing I had an auntie who'd be as glad to see me as Hyacinth was to see Perry. I could have used some hugging myself.

Finally Hyacinth freed herself from Perry and led us into her cabin. There was just one room, but it was warm and cozy and tidy. And it smelled of good things to eat. She seated us at a table in front of the fire and commenced to fix our dinner, filling three plates with beans and baked yams and the fluffiest biscuits I ever did see. The whole while she worked, she kept her eyes on Perry as if she couldn't get enough of him.

"You have the same dimple in your chin your mother had," she said softly. "The shape of your face reminds me of Lydia, too."

Hyacinth herself didn't have Lydia's prettiness. She was taller and thinner. Older, too, I reckoned. But, like Athena said, she seemed sensible enough.

"You boys eat your dinner now," Hyacinth went on. "You can tell me everything afterwards."

Perry didn't stay awake long enough to do any telling. He fell asleep at the table before he'd finished his second helping. Hyacinth picked him up and carried him to a pallet by the fire. Careful not to wake him, she covered him with a patchwork quilt. For a few moments she stood there looking down at him, her face full of woe. Then she came back to the table and turned her attention to me.

"How is it you have Perry?" she asked.

"Lydia ran away from the Widow Baxter," I explained. "But before she died, she made me promise to bring Perry to Miss Polly Baxter. She said Miss Polly was the boy's aunt and she'd help him."

"So Mr. Peregrine Baxter was Perry's father?" Something in the way she asked told me it wasn't no surprise to her. "The boy bears some resemblance to the man, I suppose."

"Lydia told me herself," I said. "She also told me his widow planned to sell her and Perry south. For spite, I reckon. When they ran away, she sent her uncle Abednego Botfield after them. Do you know him?"

"Yes, indeed, I know Colonel Botfield," Hyacinth muttered. "May his soul burn in hell for all the misery he's caused."

"Amen," I said, agreeing wholeheartedly. Then, while Hyacinth listened closely, I told her all that had happened, beginning with Lydia's death and ending with Perry's and my trip to Virginia. It seemed the story got longer every time, for there were new things to add to each telling.

Hyacinth sat still a long time after I stopped talking, her face a study of sorrow and worry. The fire burned low, and a log fell, sending a shower of sparks up the chimney. The wind rattled a branch against the closed shutters. I shivered, for the sound was like the dead knocking to come in from the dark.

Finally Hyacinth wiped her eyes with her apron and turned to me. "I haven't seen Lydia for nine years," she said. "When Mr. Peregrine took a fancy to her, he sent me to Baltimore, and he sold Mama south. He didn't want us coming between him and Lydia."

Hyacinth glared at me as if I was somehow to blame. "Lydia was only fourteen years old," she said. "A pretty child, that's what she was, foolish enough to believe his lies."

Her voice was so full of hate for Mr. Peregrine Baxter I found myself wanting to take up for the poor man. Why, I don't know. It pained me to think of him wooing Lydia when she was only a couple of years older than me. Selling her sister and mama wasn't too good either. But he'd always had a friendly greeting when I passed him on the road, and I'd never heard my uncle say a bad word about him. Besides, I'd been taught not to speak ill of the dead, who couldn't defend themselves.

"Mr. Baxter was good to Lydia and Perry," I ventured. "They had fine clothes, and they speak better than many a white person, myself included. And Lydia mourned his passing. I seen her tears myself."

"Oh, I reckon Mr. Baxter was kind enough when he was alone with the two of them," Hyacinth said. "But they were still his slaves, weren't they, to do with as he wished?"

"He meant to free them," I said. "Lydia told me so herself, but he died before he—"

Hyacinth cut me off with a scornful laugh. "That's what men like Mr. Baxter always tell slaves like Lydia. Trouble is, they never get around to filing those manumission papers." She rose to her feet, sending her shadow racing up the wall and across the ceiling. "The smartest thing Lydia ever did was run away. I just wish she'd done it sooner."

I had nothing more to say. I couldn't argue with the truth. So I just shrank down in my chair and rubbed my eyes, which were itching something fierce. Most likely because I was weary of everything. Seemed like my worries would never be over.

"Go on, lie down now," Hyacinth said in a kindlier voice, "and get some rest. You're nothing but an ignorant child yourself."

Glad to escape her sharp tongue, I curled up under the blanket beside Perry. Ignorant, my foot. I knew plenty of things. I had a half a mind to tell her so, but I thought I'd close my eyes for a second first. Just to rest a little.

CHAPTER 13

I must have been even wearier than I thought, for the next time I opened my eyes it was morning. Perry was already sitting at the table, eating oatmeal. When Hyacinth heard me stirring, she filled a bowl for me.

When we were done eating, I asked when we could meet Polly and tell her our story. I was anxious to be done with my promise. The sooner Perry was safe, the sooner I'd be free to go home.

"I think I should talk to Miss Polly first," Hyacinth said.

Perry's face scrunched with worry. "She won't send me back to the widow, will she?"

"Of course not," I spoke up. "Miss Polly's going to love you, Perry. Just you wait and see if she don't."

Hyacinth gave me a troubled look. "As I said, Jesse, I'll speak to Miss Polly first thing this morning."

"But—"

Hyacinth pressed her finger to my mouth to silence me. "Jesse, I'm telling you to keep yourself out of this. I'm due at the big house. While I'm gone, I want you and Perry to stay here in the cabin. No one must see either one of you. I can't risk folks asking questions."

"But somebody already saw us," Perry piped up, worried as usual. "We knocked on a door last night, and the woman there told us which cabin was yours."

Hyacinth frowned. "Which door did you knock on?"

"The first one we come to," I said, "the cabin at the top of the hill."

"That would be Esmerelda," Hyacinth said. "I'll see her at the big house and tell her to keep quiet about you two." Giving Perry a kiss, she went to the door and opened it cautiously. The morning sun slanted in, bringing bird songs and fresh smells with it.

"Remember what I said," she warned. "Don't let anyone see you. Don't talk to anyone. Wait here for me."

When the door closed behind her, the ray of sunlight vanished, leaving the cabin gray and quiet. For an hour or two, Perry and I amused ourselves playing with a set of checkers we found. But as time passed, we got more and more restless. I kept peeking out the door, looking for Hyacinth. There was never a soul to be seen.

At last I said, "I reckon all the slaves are working somewhere, Perry. Why don't we sneak outside for a spell? I can't stand sitting around all day doing nothing."

At first Perry said no, we had to do what Hyacinth

said, but I kept at him till I wore him down. We opened the door and looked both ways. Listened, too. Saw nothing, heard nothing. Off we ran, quick as rabbits, and plunged into the woods.

We followed a path uphill, glad to be outside in the fresh air. In a few minutes we found ourselves on a bluff high above the Potomac. The ferry was just below, no bigger than a child's toy, heading across the river. On the Maryland side a train was chugging along, hauling a long line of cars. Everything looked so peaceful it was hard to believe a war was shaping up. Like those men I'd heard talking at the ferry landing, I expected the whole thing would be settled soon—which meant I'd never get a chance to be a soldier.

Maybe it was just as well, for I still hadn't decided what side to fight for, North or South. I reckoned I was leaning toward the Union, though, mainly because Colonel Abednego Botfield was for the Confederacy. Now that I knew a bit more about the issue, I didn't want to fight for slavers either. It seemed I was becoming a Yankee slow but sure, which would most likely rile Uncle Philemon—if I ever saw him again.

Perry and I fooled around on the bluff, tossing stones into the river. After a while, we heard someone coming and hid behind a tree. Soon Miss Polly herself came strolling into sight, carrying a parasol to shield her face from the sun. She had a little spotted dog with her, the kind that's good for nothing but yapping—which was exactly what it commenced to do. I reckoned it had caught a whiff of strangers lurking in the woods.

"This is our chance, Perry," I whispered. "We got Miss Polly all to ourselves. We can tell her everything right this minute."

He grabbed my arm to stop me from barging out from behind the tree. "Remember what Hyacinth said, Jesse. We aren't supposed to talk to anyone. Why, we aren't even supposed to be outside the cabin."

"Now, listen here," I started to say but at that moment the dog found us. It commenced to dance around our ankles, raising the shrillest racket I ever heard.

"Lady, come back here at once!" Miss Polly called. But the nasty little critter paid its mistress no mind. Without warning, it nipped my ankle, causing me to holler, more out of surprise than pain.

"Who's there?" Miss Polly cried.

Motioning Perry to stay put, I stepped out from behind the tree, dragging the dog along with me. It had a grip on me and didn't plan to let go no matter how hard I shook my leg.

At the sight of me, Polly took a few steps backward, as if I might be dangerous.

"Call your dog off," I begged. "I don't mean you no harm. I just want to talk to you, that's all."

"Lady, come here," Miss Polly said. The dog kept right on growling, its teeth buried in my ankle as if I was the daintiest morsel it had tasted in a long while.

Miss Polly came closer and yanked the dog away

from me. My ankle was bleeding, but she cuddled that cussed little dog as if I'd attacked it instead of the other way around. "What are you doing on my uncle's property?" she asked.

Since she seemed a trifle skittish, I thought it best to tell her straight off why I was here. "My name's Jesse Sherman, and I've come a long way to bring you a message from your friend Lydia."

Polly looked puzzled. "Lydia? Lydia who? I don't recollect a friend named Lydia."

Now I was puzzled. "You must remember Lydia," I said. "She was your brother's house girl down at Baxter's Folly."

"Oh, yes, of course, that Lydia," Polly said. "I didn't realize you were speaking of a slave."

I was getting a bad feeling about Miss Polly Baxter, but I told myself I'd startled her, and that's why she was talking so silly.

"Why would Lydia send a boy like you to me?" Polly went on, obviously put off by my appearance. "I don't understand."

"Well, she aimed to come see you herself," I said, "only she—"

"But Lydia's a slave," Polly interrupted. "How could she travel all this way?"

"She ran away," I said, "and—"

Polly looked like she was about to faint. "Why on earth did she do such a foolish thing? My poor late brother was so fond of that girl. If he'd lived, he would have freed her, you know."

She shook her head as if to clear her mind of vexatious thoughts. "I can't hide Lydia here, if that's what you're asking. My uncle wouldn't tolerate it, not if she's run away, but if she needs money, clothing—"

"I'm afraid Lydia don't need any of those things now," I broke in. "The truth is she's dead. She—"

Polly turned so pale I feared she might faint. "Lydia's dead? Oh, dear, no, not Lydia." She began to weep into a pretty little handkerchief.

"That's why I'm here," I told her. "Lydia asked me to bring you her son, in hope you'd—"

Polly lowered her handkerchief and stared at me as if I'd taken leave of my senses. "Lydia had no child. Why, I saw her at Christmastime. Surely she would have told me . . . "

While Miss Polly babbled, I leaned around the tree and beckoned to Perry. I figured as soon as she saw him she'd realize Mr. Peregrine was his daddy. Hadn't several people noticed his resemblance already?

Perry came out slowly, dragging his feet. Scowling at me, he said, "Hyacinth told us not to—"

But Polly hushed him with a cry. With tears running down her cheeks, she reached out for him just as I'd thought she would. "Oh, you look just like your mother," she exclaimed. "Right down to the dimple on your chin."

Perry came closer, but not close enough for Polly to touch him. He stopped a few feet away and stared at her.

I nudged Perry nearer to Polly. "Show her the locket your mama gave you."

He stuck his hand deep down in his pocket and pulled out the tiny heart, its chain tangled and knotted. He held out his palm so Polly could see.

She leaned over Perry's hand and stared at the locket. "What's that?"

"Open it," I told her.

Polly took the locket and pried it apart with her fingernail. "It's a picture of Peregrine," she said, "and Lydia. Where did you get this?"

Though Polly was asking Perry, I answered for him. "His mama gave it to him before she died. She said you'd know the meaning of it."

Polly stared hard at the tiny pictures in the locket. "I don't understand," she whispered. Her face turned bright pink as if it embarrassed her to be so slow witted.

I was at a loss now. For all I knew, Polly had no notion of how such things came about between men and women. She'd lived a sheltered city life. Nobody had ever put her in charge of a bull or asked her to help at calving time. I looked at Perry. He just stood there, his face as blank as Polly's. Most likely he'd never done any barnyard chores either.

"Tell Polly who your daddy was," I urged him.

Perry drew a little closer to me. "You tell her, Jesse," he begged.

I cleared my throat and looked Polly in the eye. "Like you said," I started, "your brother was powerful fond of Lydia. More fond than he ought to have been, with him being married and all."

I paused to see if she was catching on. If she was, the girl gave no sign of it. I could feel my own face turning as red as hers, but I went on with my little speech. "Well, the long and short of it is this, Miss Polly—Perry here is your brother's son."

Polly drew back from Perry and turned pale. "That can't be true. Peregrine would never—"

"Don't you see how close he resembles your brother?"

Polly glanced at Perry and burst into tears. Pressing her little hanky to her face, she flung the locket on the ground. With Lady yapping at her side, she began to run toward the big house.

I chased after her and grabbed her arm, jerking her to a stop. Though Lady nipped at me, I seized the girl's wrists and held her tight. "I don't know what you aim to do," I said, "but don't you dare tell anyone you seen us. The Widow Baxter hates Perry for being who he is. I swear she'd kill him if she got the chance."

Polly began to tremble as if she feared I was about to strike her, but I felt no pity for her. All I could think of was Lydia and how sorely Miss Polly Baxter had deceived her. It seemed Hyacinth knew a sight more about white folks than I did, and I wished with all my heart I'd listened to her.

"Let her go," Perry begged me. "Let her go before someone comes and catches us." He began crying, too.

"I'm sorry I can't help Perry," Polly whimpered through her tears. "Truly I am. I was fond of Lydia, but my father would never claim kinship to a slave. He'd return the boy to Henrietta. By law, she's his rightful owner, and my father believes in the law above all else."

"If you're scared to help your own nephew," I said, "swear not to say a word about him to anyone in your uncle's house." To show her I meant what I said, I squeezed her soft white wrists. "That's all I ask. We'll leave like we came, nice and quiet."

"I promise I won't tell a soul," Polly sobbed. "But you must go this very minute. If Uncle Cornelius finds you, there's no telling what he'll do. He's even stricter than Father when it comes to runaways. And he has company from Baltimore, men loyal to the Cause."

She turned, still crying, and fled like the very devil was chasing her. This time I let her go. I hoped she'd calm down before anyone saw her and asked what the trouble was. She didn't strike me as the sort who'd make up a good lie.

I turned to Perry, but he was scowling at me through his tears, fairly shaking with anger. "Now see what you've done," he hollered. "What am I to do? Where am I to go? Oh, why didn't you let me die in the woods with Mama?"

With that, the child took off running, crashing into the woods, heading back to the cabin as fast and reckless as he could go. I ran after him and brought him to a stop. If he hadn't been crying, I might have punched his nose, for it made me mad to be blamed for the way things had turned out. After all, it was his mama's idea to come to Miss Polly Baxter, not mine. I'd just done what Lydia had asked. Kept my promise and then some, for Lydia hadn't said nothing about coming all the way to Virginia.

"Listen here, Perry," I began in a gruff voice for I was more upset than I cared to show. "We got to think things out. Maybe Hyacinth—"

"You should have done what she told you!" Perry cut in. "When she finds out we talked to Polly, she'll be mad. What if she sends us away?"

"Hyacinth won't do that," I said. "She's your mama's sister." But as I spoke, it occurred to me Hyacinth could very well send me packing. I wasn't no kin to her. The Lord only knew how I'd find my way home from here.

Perry scowled at the ground. It was clear he was having another one of his spells of silence and would say nothing more till he was ready.

I walked a little farther into the woods and sat on the trunk of a fallen tree. Maybe if I left him alone, he'd get over his mood and be friendly again. After a long while, I heard the leaves rustle behind me. I didn't turn around. If Perry wanted to talk to me, he'd have to start the conversation.

He sat down on the tree beside me, not real close, but I could hear him breathing. More time passed. A woodpecker hammered away at a dead branch over our heads. A mockingbird ran through his notes, singing them over and over as if he was practicing for some great event. A train whistle blew across the river. But Perry said nothing, and neither did I.

"I been thinking," Perry announced at last.

I peeled bark off a twig like it was a task of some importance and waited for him to go on.

"Mama trusted Polly and you," he said slowly. "She was wrong about Polly, but you came all this way with me just because she asked you to. You could have gone back home anytime."

I looked at him. His face was streaked with tears and dirt, but he was trying to smile, even though his chin wobbled a little.

"More than once I wanted to run off and leave you by your lonesome," I confessed. "But every time I thought about going home, I remembered your mama and how I'd sworn to keep you safe. So here I am and there you are, and what we're going to do now I just don't know."

"I suppose you're sorry you made that promise," Perry said, scowling again. "Most likely you can't wait to be rid of me."

I went back to peeling my twig while I considered what he'd said. "Truth to tell, Perry," I spoke up at last, "I've grown used to you, though I must say you ain't always the best of companions."

"I guess I'm used to you, too, Jesse," Perry said in a low voice, "but you make me awful mad sometimes." He sighed and moved a little closer to me.

We sat there a while without talking, but it was a peaceful silence this time. I judged it to be about three o'clock, which meant about four hours to go before dark. A long time to wait with an empty belly and nothing to do.

When I got tired of sitting, I slid off the log and reached out to help Perry down. He hesitated a second, but then he took my hand and jumped to the ground beside me.

Perry picked up a long stick and whacked the bushes. "Let's pretend this is the Green Wood," he said, "and we're Robin Hood's men, hiding here to rob the rich and give to the poor."

I looked at him with some perplexity, for I had never heard of Robin Hood or the Green Wood.

"Don't you know the story of Robin and his Merry Men?" Perry asked. "Papa was reading it to me before he died, so I never heard how it ends."

I stared at him in some surprise. "Mr. Peregrine read stories to you?"

Perry whacked the bushes again. "Papa used to come to Mama and me late at night," he said, "and sit by the fire with me on his lap, reading stories from a big book. He taught me my letters and my numbers, too."

I remembered what Hyacinth had told me about Mr. Peregrine Baxter, but I didn't say nothing. Sooner or later Perry would hear her side of things, but it wasn't my place to speak up against the man.

"Sounds like Mr. Peregrine was a good daddy to you," I said, thinking he'd done more for Perry than my uncle ever did for me.

"Papa was only there at nighttime," Perry said in a

low voice. "In the daytime he never paid me the least notice. Mama told me I wasn't to talk to him unless he spoke first. And I was never, never to call him Papa anywhere but in our quarters when there was nobody else around."

Judging by the look on Perry's face, I reckoned it might be good to talk of something else. "Tell me about Robin Hood," I said. "What kind of story is it?"

"Well, it happened in England way back a long time ago in the days of knights and ladies and noble deeds," Perry began. "Robin Hood was cheated out of his land by the Sheriff of Nottingham, so he hid in the Green Wood and became chief of a band of outlaws. But they weren't bad. They stole from the rich and gave to the poor, which was a good thing to do."

Perry talked on and on, telling of high deeds till my head was full of pictures of the olden days. I'd never heard such tales in my life, and when he fell silent, I yearned to hear the ending as much as he did.

"It would be a fine game to play," I said. "I can be Robin Hood and you—"

"Why should you be Robin Hood?" Perry asked. "I told you about him, so I should be Robin Hood."

"But I'm the biggest," I said.

"That's why you should be Little John," Perry said.

"Little? Why—"

"Little John is called 'Little' because he's so big," Perry explained.

That didn't make no sense to me. If I was big, I'd

want to be called big, not little. I eyed Perry suspiciously. "Was Little John as brave as Robin Hood?"

Perry nodded. "He started out to be Robin's enemy, but then, after they had a fight, they became the very best of friends and did noble deeds together."

"Well, I'm calling myself Big John," I said. "It sounds a heap more sensible."

Perry looked as if he might put up a fuss but changed his mind. "We can make bows and arrows from sticks," he said. "And then we can hunt deer just like Robin and Big John."

It took us a while to make the bows. We used grape vine for the string, but it didn't work too good. If we pulled too hard, the whole contraption fell apart. But we stalked through the forest anyway, ever watchful for our enemies.

After a while, we spotted three white men coming along a trail. I recognized Mr. Cornelius Baxter, but the other two were strangers. They carried guns and their faces were grim.

"Rich merchants of Nottingham," Perry whispered.

Before they saw us, we ducked into the bushes and aimed our arrows at them. They passed by our hiding place, unaware of how close they were to death.

"I reckon it was a Yankee soldier," Mr. Baxter was saying. "They've been known to accost innocent young ladies like my niece."

His friend spat in the dirt. "Most likely the coward's run back across the river by now."

"It's a pitiful shame a young lady ain't safe on her own land these days," said the third.

"Don't you worry, Henry. Once the Virginia army gets itself together, we won't see any Yankees on our soil."

"Let's go back to the house," Mr. Baxter suggested. "I could use a drink of whiskey 'long about now."

The men walked on and the woods closed in behind them, quiet except for birds.

"They're hunting us," Perry whispered. "Polly must have told after all."

"They were looking for a Yankee, not two boys," I said slowly. "Maybe Polly came home all in an uproar and her uncle thought it was a soldier that scared her. Maybe she didn't say nothing at all about us. Maybe she just let him think what he liked."

Perry frowned. "You're taking up for her because she's pretty," he said. "That's all."

Dropping our bows and arrows on the ground, we began making our way back to the cabin. The game was over. It was time to face Hyacinth.

CHAPTER 14

Hyacinth was waiting for us. She opened her cabin door and dragged us inside fast. "What have you done, Jesse?" she asked. "I told you to stay inside and wait for me, but you ran off and did just what I warned you not to do!" She was so mad she was practically shooting fire at me.

"I'm sorry," I said, but I don't think she even noticed or cared what I had to say.

"You upset Miss Polly so bad she's taken to her bed," Hyacinth went on. "I meant to talk to her before she went out for her afternoon walk, but her mother kept me busy ironing and mending and doing for her. By the time I was free, Miss Polly was running in the back door, out of her head with grief and fear, throwing the whole household into an uproar."

"Did she tell about seeing us?" Perry asked.

"Bless her heart," Hyacinth said, "Miss Polly kept

quiet about you and Jesse. Everyone thought she'd seen a stranger in the woods. Her uncle and some of his friends went out hunting for him, convinced she'd met up with a Yankee spy."

"We saw those men," Perry spoke up, "but they didn't see us 'cause we were hiding."

On hearing that, Hyacinth sank down at the table, her head in her hands. "Lord, Lord," she prayed, "why did these children have to come here now?"

Perry began to cry, taking the words to mean she didn't want him. Turning to him, Hyacinth hugged him tight. "Oh, Perry, don't cry," she said. "It's just that you couldn't have picked a worse time to come to me. I told you Mr. Baxter is selling arms to the Confederates. The man supplying the rifles is Colonel Botfield himself. He's up at the big house now, along with a Confederate officer."

Perry turned pale, and I felt my knees go weak. Like I'd suspected, Colonel Botfield and me were part of the same story. No matter where I went, that devil was close behind.

"We can't stay here," I said. "What if Polly takes a notion to tell her uncle about us? Or just lets something slip by accident? The colonel will be on our trail in a flash."

Hyacinth opened the shutter and peeked outside. It was dusk but not yet dark. Candles shone from the windows of the big house, and sounds of merriment drifted our way. Though I couldn't be absolutely sure, I thought I detected Colonel Botfield's laughter.

Hyacinth closed the shutter and latched it. "You boys sit down and eat your supper," she said. "We'll be doing some traveling later tonight."

"Where—" I asked, but she silenced me with a sharp look.

"Just do as I say, Jesse." Without another word, Hyacinth ladled rabbit stew into three bowls and set them on the table. I burned my tongue on the first spoonful because I couldn't wait to get that hot food in my stomach. When I asked for another helping, Hyacinth shook her head.

"But there's more in the pot," I said, too hungry to remember my manners.

"That's for someone else," Hyacinth said in a low voice.

"Who?" I asked, puzzled by her secretive manner.

"Don't ask any more questions," she said, as if I'd vexed her in some way.

"But—"

Hyacinth shook her head. "What did I say, Jesse?"

It was clear she meant me to hush, so I did. After that, nobody said anything at all. It was so quiet I could hear the wind stirring the trees outside the cabin and the crackle and pop of the fire on the hearth. Perry was falling asleep over his empty plate again, head nodding, eyes closing, but Hyacinth sat up straight and tense, studying the flames, her face sharp and bony. As for me,

I stared at the pot and wondered who was to get the stew I hungered for.

Suddenly Hyacinth looked at Perry. "Why don't you go on to bed, honey?" she asked gently.

He slid off his chair and went to Hyacinth. I watched him kiss her good night as natural as if he'd already begun to think of her as his mama. Then, nodding to me, he crawled under the quilt.

Hyacinth watched him for a few moments and then turned to me. "My sister trusted you with the life of her only child," she said in a low voice. "Now I have to decide if I can trust you."

I guessed she was still mad about what I'd done earlier. Truth to tell, I wished with my all heart I'd stayed in the cabin like she'd told me to. But as both Uncle Philemon and Delia had said more than once, I didn't have the sense I was born with.

"I'm sorry about speaking to Polly like I done," I said. "I swear I'll do what you say from now on."

She studied me a long while without saying a word. I kept my eyes on hers so she'd know I was telling the truth. Outside the cabin, the wind picked up a little, and I heard an owl hoot close by.

Hyacinth glanced at Perry as if to make sure he was truly asleep. "A group of runaways is hiding in the woods north of here," she said slowly, keeping her voice real low. "Two women, a man, and a baby. All but one have traveled a long way, and I've been feeding them to build up their strength. We planned to leave for Ohio next week, but now I'm afraid to wait that long."

Suddenly she reached across the table and seized my hand. I'd never met a woman with a grip as strong as hers. "You'll have to come with us, Jesse. I can't risk leaving you here. I know where you were born and who brought you up. I know what you've been taught."

I started to speak, but she hushed me. "They're all rebel lovers on the Shore. Why, if it wasn't for Mr. Lincoln's army, the whole bunch of them would be in the Confederacy by now, including your uncle, Mr. Philemon Sherman."

"Not me." I found my voice at last. "I wouldn't belong to no nation that has Colonel Abednego Botfield in it."

Hyacinth eyed me. She hadn't eased her grip on my wrist. Trying not to flinch, I said, "I swear I'll never betray you. You think I brought Perry all this way to see him get caught?"

"Just be sure you remember that," Hyacinth said. "White folks have a way of going back on their word."

It cut me to the heart to hear her speak so distrustfully, but there was no denying such things happened. "Didn't I keep my promise to Lydia as best I could?"

Hyacinth reached out and patted my hand in a kindly way. "I'm sorry for doubting you, Jesse. But my own mama is with those runaways, and I can't take any chances on her being caught."

"Your mama?" I stared at her as the full meaning of her words sunk in. "Perry's granny?"

Hyacinth nodded. "I been searching for her such a long time, asking every slave I meet if they've seen her. Not long ago I got word where she was. As soon as Polly and I arrived here, I sent a message to Mama telling her I was at Mr. Cornelius Baxter's place, close to her. She ran the first chance she got. Lord, it was good to see her. Nine years is a long while to be apart."

Hyacinth broke off talking and stared into the fire. "Mama doesn't know Lydia's dead. Nor does she know about Perry." She sighed and shook her head. "Now's not the time to sit here thinking sad thoughts. We have to get ourselves ready to go."

Getting to her feet, she began to gather things for the trip. "Make a bedroll with your blankets, Jesse, and help Perry do the same."

Perry woke in some confusion. "Why are you taking the blankets?" he asked, grabbing for one. "I'm cold, Jesse."

Hyacinth hushed him and blew out the candle. The fire had burned itself down to embers so the cabin was almost as dark as the woods outside. "We're leaving here," she told Perry, "so we must be as quiet as quiet can be."

"Where are we going?" Perry asked, suddenly fearful.

"Someplace we'll be safe," Hyacinth whispered. "Safe and free. Just like your mama wanted."

"But it's dark outside. It's still nighttime." Perry looked at me. "Is the colonel coming after us?"

I shook my head. "Don't fret, Perry. The colonel don't know nothing. Just do what Hyacinth says."

Still worried, Perry let Hyacinth take his hand and lead him to the cabin door. I followed, carrying the blanket roll on my back. Once we were outside, we heard men laughing and talking in the big house. It gave me shivers to think how close the colonel was. I prayed he wouldn't come to the window and see Perry and me skulking past in the shadows.

Hyacinth strode into the woods, carrying a huge basket on her back. Perry was right behind her. I hurried after them, struggling with the bedroll.

Dark as it was, Hyacinth never hesitated. I reckoned she'd been this way before, taking food to her mama and others. We climbed one hill after another, going higher and higher with every step, following a path that wound round rocks and trees. I was soon gasping for breath, bent nearly double under the weight of the bedroll, but Hyacinth kept up a steady pace. Though every one of my muscles ached, her long skinny legs never seemed to tire.

At long last we reached level ground, high atop a ridge above the river. Across the water in Maryland, I could make out the watch fires of Federal army camps. They shone like tiny stars fallen from the sky onto the black earth—hundreds of them, it seemed.

Hyacinth looked at them. "For every Yankee fire you see on that side of the river, there's a rebel fire on this side. We got to be quiet so as not to alarm the sentries."

The thought of armed rebels all around us scared me some. Did they ask questions first or did they just shoot? And if they did ask questions, what would we answer?

"How much farther do we have to go?" Perry whispered.

"Downhill a ways," Hyacinth said. "They're hiding in a cave halfway to the river."

Downhill sounded better than uphill, but as soon as we started, I found I was wrong. The bedroll threw my balance off, and I was forever grabbing at bushes and trees to keep myself from tumbling straight down into the river. A whole new bunch of muscles came into play as well, and I began to ache in places I didn't know I had.

Just when I thought I couldn't take another step, Hyacinth motioned me to stop. "You boys wait here," she whispered. "I'll tell them you're coming."

In a trice, she'd disappeared into the trees, leaving Perry and me alone. He turned to me, his face a blur in the dark. "What if Mr. Baxter and the colonel come after us?" he whispered.

"They won't do that," I blustered. "From the sounds of it, they was too busy funning themselves playing cards and drinking." But I found myself looking over my shoulder anyway, worrying about the colonel.

"I wish I had Mama's knife," Perry said.

I wished he did, too, but before I could say so, Hyacinth came creeping back so quiet she scared me half out of my skin. "Come along now," she whispered.

We followed her into a thicket of brambles at the

foot of a rocky cliff. The thorns scratched at my face like tiny claws, and I felt my shirt rip once or twice. When we got through the prickers, Hyacinth led us into a tiny hole that seemed a likely place for a fox den. It was the darkest place I'd ever been. I couldn't see nothing, not even Perry, who was just ahead of me. The air had a cold, damp edge to it, like a musty cellar. I imagined graves had a similar smell. I wriggled after Perry as fast I could go, getting his foot in my face more than once.

All of a sudden we came around a bend and crawled out into a space as big as a church, lit by a small fire. I got to my feet and stared around me in wonder. I'd heard tell of caves, but I'd never seen one before, so I had no way of knowing whether this was special or just ordinary. The rock walls slanted up and up, higher than the firelight could show. Long pointed things like stone icicles hung down from somewhere above, and others grew up from the floor. Some met and formed pillars. The sight fair took my breath away. I felt like I'd come to another world hidden away underground.

All at once someone coughed. A woman by the fire got to her feet. "It's him, isn't it?" she asked Hyacinth, but her eyes were on Perry. "Lydia's son."

Hyacinth nudged Perry forward, but he'd gone shy on her. Like a little child, he clung to her skirt and stared at the woman.

She was about Athena and Delia's age, I thought. Lean and pleasant-featured. No gray in her hair, no wrinkles in her skin. Despite her raggedy clothes, she was proud in the way she held herself. In fact, she put me in mind of Lydia standing there in the woods, tall and straight, her belly busting with that baby. I knew she just had to be Perry's granny.

Reaching toward Perry, the woman said, "Come closer, boy. Let me get a better look at you."

Hyacinth gave Perry a firmer nudge. "Go on," she said. "Can't you guess who that is?"

Perry glanced at Hyacinth and then took a few steps toward the woman. "Did you know my mama?" he asked.

Catching hold of Perry's hand, she drew him close. "Lydia was my daughter, darling, and you're my grandson."

When he heard that, Perry flung his arms about the woman's neck. The two of them held each other tight.

Watching them, I'm ashamed to say I felt a twinge of the same old jealousy I'd felt when Hyacinth made such a fuss over Perry. Nobody in this world loved me the way his granny and his auntie loved him, and that was a fact. Even considering what he'd gone through, it seemed he was luckier than I was.

After a while Perry's granny looked at me. "Are you sure we can trust that white boy, Hyacinth?"

"I told you, he brought Perry all this way," Hyacinth said. "He's risked his own life for the child, all on account of the promise he made to Lydia."

Perry's granny came closer and studied me hard. I

done my best to bear her scrutiny so she wouldn't think I had something to hide. Finally she said, "I hear you've made an enemy of Abednego Botfield."

"He hates me on account I helped Perry and Lydia," I said. "The last time I saw him he told me he'd be my death."

Perry's granny relaxed somewhat. "Let's hope Abednego's wrong about you," she said. "For I aim to be *his* death."

A man stepped out of the shadows, a tall, spare fellow without any meat on his bones. "Maror," he said to Perry's granny, "shouldn't we eat and be on our way?"

Without saying a word, a young woman joined him. Her dress hung raggedy from her thin shoulders. In her arms was a baby about a year old. They both had a weak and sickly look.

The man put his arm around her and led her to the fire. "Sit and have your supper, Pearl. There's a long path ahead. You got to build your strength."

While Hyacinth dished out the stew, I watched Perry's granny, Maror. She kept him close to her, sharing her food with him and fussing over him. Perry smiled and laughed, shedding his cares faster than a snake sheds its skin. Although things hadn't turned out quite as Lydia planned, I believed she'd be happy to see her son and her mama and her sister together.

By the time we were ready to leave the cave, I'd learned the man's name was Thomas. He and Pearl had both come through the mountains from North Carolina with their baby. They'd met Maror in Virginia and joined up with her.

"It's a little easier now," he told me. "White folks ain't got the time or inclination to chase every runaway slave like they used to."

Instead of leaving through the tiny tunnel, Hyacinth led us out another way, lighting our path with a torch. We could stand up straight, but it scared me to be so far under the ground. Passageways led off this way and that, disappearing into the darkness. There was no telling what manner of beasts might be waiting around the next bend—wolves, bears, or even the colonel himself. Why, the gates of hell could be down one of those tunnels.

At last we started turning upward. The tunnel shrunk in size, so we had to crawl again, slithering on our bellies like snakes. I glimpsed light ahead, just a glimmer of moon and stars shining over Hyacinth's shoulders. We came out on a ledge above the Potomac River. Never had I been so glad to see the night sky.

"How far have we come?" I asked Hyacinth.

"Baxter's place is five miles back, maybe more, maybe less." She pointed across the river. "We're aiming to come ashore in the woods above New Berlin and make our way west. There are some folks along the way who will help us, Quakers mainly, some Methodists. If we make it to Ohio we ought to be safe."

Hyacinth led us down a winding trail, even steeper than the one we'd traveled before. It was so dark we had to feel our way along, slipping on loose stones every now and then and grabbing at bushes and roots. I was glad it was dark and I couldn't see how high up we were. Heights made me dizzy, and I feared falling.

At the river's edge, Hyacinth told us to wait where we were. "A Quaker man lives up around the bend," she said. "Samuel's got a boat to take us across. I'll go fetch him."

The rest of us huddled together in the dark. Maror kept Perry close to her side. Pearl cuddled the baby and tried to hush its whimpers. Thomas stood beside me, keeping watch. Nobody said a word. We just stood there, listening to the river gurgle and hoping nothing would go wrong.

CHAPTER 15

But, of course, things did go wrong. Not long after Hyacinth left, we heard horses' hooves on the rocks above us. A familiar voice shouted, "I tell you she must have come this way, seeking to cross the river."

Perry grabbed my arm. "It's him, Jesse," he whispered, "it's the colonel coming after us."

I done my best to hush him, for it seemed the men had stopped directly overhead. Thomas looked grim, and Pearl rocked the baby. Luckily for all of us, he seemed to be sleeping peacefully.

"I can't think what got into the wench," Mr. Baxter said. "My brother never said a word about her being the sort to run off."

"Don't worry, Cornelius," Colonel Botfield said. "We'll find her. She can't have gone far."

A third man said something about wasting time

pursuing one runaway slave, but neither Mr. Baxter nor Colonel Botfield paid him any mind. It was clear they'd had way too much to drink and were wild to chase after anything that ran.

In a second or two, they were off again. We listened to the horses' hooves, trying to figure which way they'd gone, but none of us could tell for sure.

"Polly must have told after all," Perry whispered.

"Maybe not," I said. "It could be they sent for Hyacinth to fetch them something. When they saw she was gone, they set out after her."

Perry gave me a look that plainly said I was a fool to make excuses for a white girl. Could be he was right. If there was one thing I'd learned since leaving home, it was to doubt my own intelligence.

Not long after the men rode away, a boat no bigger than a dinghy came floating quietly toward us, with a man at the oars and Hyacinth seated in the back.

A few yards from shore, Samuel motioned to us. "I can't come any closer," he called softly. "The current's too swift."

Holding tight to Perry's hand, Maror followed Thomas and Pearl into the river. I came last. Even though it was May, the water was cold. It wasn't quite waist-deep on me, but it was almost up to Perry's chest. The current tugged at my legs, threatening to pull them out from under me.

Hyacinth leaned out and took Pearl's baby. Thomas boosted his wife into the boat and climbed in after her.

I watched him haul Perry in like a fresh caught fish. Maror clambered over the side, weighed down by her skirt. Just as Thomas reached for me, a voice rang out from somewhere above us.

"There she is—and she ain't alone! Stop them before they get across the river!"

Colonel Abednego Botfield had caught up with me once again. A rifle sounded, but the shot went wide. It was still dark and the boat was moving, so I had every hope no one would be hit.

"Hang on to the side," Thomas told me.

The current was already catching the boat, moving it farther from shore. Samuel bent to the oars, and I clung to the side as tight as I could. All the time bullets whizzed past, buzzing like deadly wasps, and hissing into the water. It seemed I'd joined the war after all.

Suddenly Samuel dropped the oars and slumped forward with a groan. Thomas grabbed for the oars, but they slipped out of the locks before he got them. With nobody to steer, the current carried the boat downstream, spinning this way and that like a child's toy.

That's when I lost my grip on the side. The water carried me away, pulling me under and then spitting me out. I gasped and sputtered, kicking my feet and thrashing my arms, doing my best to swim. It was a skill I hadn't learned too good. Worse yet, I'd never tried it in water like this. Where I came from, the rivers moved slow and easy. I'd heard of rapids, but this was my first experience with them. I hoped I'd live to tell about it.

Just when I thought I was done for, I managed to grab hold of a tree hanging over the water. It was all I could do to keep my grip, for the river was running fast and strong and I was weak with cold. Hanging on to the tree, I managed to pull myself along its trunk, hand over hand, till my feet touched bottom.

Half drowned, I climbed out of the river and lay on the ground, breathing hard and shivering. My wet clothes chilled me through and through. I didn't have the gumption to get up. I just wanted to stay where I was. At least I was safe.

But not for long. Somewhere in the trees, not far off, I heard men shouting, the colonel's voice amongst them. I pressed myself flat, and they galloped past not three feet away, so close the ground shook under the horses' hooves.

"Most likely the boat'll hit the rocks up ahead," the colonel hollered. "I know I hit two of them, must have killed at least one."

I got up real slow and followed the sounds of the men and horses along the river. What I was going to do I had no idea, but I hoped something would come to me.

The woods thinned out ahead, and I ducked behind a tree to see what I could see. The sun was starting to come up behind a wall of thick gray clouds, bringing no warmth with it and not much light. I made out the shape of the boat in the water. Like the colonel predicted, it had run aground on the rocks close to shore.

A dark figure slumped over the side, most likely Samuel, the Quaker man, clearly dead. The three women huddled together. Pearl held her baby tight, but I saw no sign of Perry or Thomas.

"Where's the other man?" Colonel Botfield hollered at the women.

"Dead," Maror answered. "The boat tipped, and he fell out."

"I told you I got him." The colonel sounded mighty pleased with himself, but I felt sick.

The big question was Perry. Could I have been right about Polly keeping her mouth shut? It had been dark when we piled into that boat. If the colonel hadn't known to look for Perry and me, most likely he wouldn't have spotted us. But that still didn't tell me where the boy was. Or even if he was alive. For all I knew I'd brought him all this way just to have him drown in the river. Thinking about it was enough to make me cry. But not now. Too much was happening.

"Come on ashore, sweetheart," the colonel called to Maror. "It's a pure delight to see you again."

Maror stopped, still ankle deep in water. "It's a pity I can't say the same of you, Abednego. I hoped you were dead and buried by now, down in hell swapping tales with the devil."

"Oh, now," he said, "there's no need to talk so ugly, Susie."

"I don't answer to that name anymore," Maror said. Without looking at him again, she took Hyacinth's hand and led her out of the water. Pearl followed, still hugging the baby to her breast.

Undiscouraged, the colonel went right up to Maror and grinned that evil grin of his. "No matter what you call yourself, you'll always be Susie to me," he said.

"Her name is Maror," Hyacinth put in, "to remind herself of the bitterness of slavery."

"Is that right?" The colonel pulled a cigar out of his pocket and lit it. "Susie always did love her Bible stories."

Still grinning, he said to Maror, "I hear you ran away from my old friend's plantation. Why don't I escort you back there? I swear you're just as pretty as ever, darling."

She gave him a look so hateful it's a wonder he didn't catch fire and burn to ashes. "You lay one hand on me, Abednego, and I'll kill you."

Colonel Botfield threw back his head and laughed. "Ain't she a peach, Lieutenant Colston?" he asked the Confederate. "I never met a wench with more spirit."

The young lieutenant had been standing off to the side, watching the goings-on with a worried look. "I thought I was here to buy rifles," he said, "not to go chasing after slaves."

"When I see valuable property getting into a boat, I figure it's my duty to stop them," Colonel Botfield said.

"The rifles will keep, Colston," Mr. Baxter put in. "Neither you nor those Yankees across the river seem all that anxious to start shooting each other, anyways."

The lieutenant put his foot in the stirrup and swung himself into the saddle. "I don't have time to waste," he said. "Either we return to the house and continue the negotiations or I go back to camp. Baltimore's full of men willing to sell arms to us."

"You'll have trouble finding rifles as good as ours," Colonel Botfield replied, just as cool as he could be. Seizing Maror's arm, he said. "Let's go, Susie. No more of your sass now. Enough's enough."

At the same time, Mr. Baxter dragged Hyacinth from Maror's side. "Behave yourself," he said. "My brother won't take kindly to the news of your attempted escape."

Hyacinth paid him no mind. While Pearl cowered at the river's edge, she and Maror fought those two men, kicking, slapping, and scratching. When the colonel hit Maror hard enough to knock her down, the lieutenant shook his head and turned his horse away. Nobody but me noticed he was leaving.

Just as I was about to crash out of the bushes to help Maror and Hyacinth, gunshots rang out on all sides. It all happened so fast I could scarcely take it in. One minute, Mr. Baxter and the colonel were struggling with the women. The next, Mr. Baxter cried out and fell to the ground. Colonel Botfield let go of Maror and grabbed his rifle, but before he got a chance to shoot, he caught a bullet himself. Leaving Mr. Baxter where he'd fallen, the old devil flung himself on his horse and galloped off into the morning mist.

At the same moment, the three women ran into the woods. Before I had a chance to join them, a passel of rebels came riding out of the trees with a passel of Yankees on their tails, shooting and yelling and full of murderous intent.

The rebels came to a halt at the river's edge and took a stand in a grove of spindly willow trees. I glimpsed Lieutenant Colston among them. He must have ridden back to his men at just about the worst time he could have picked.

Not ten feet from me, the Yankees charged out of the woods, still shooting and yelling. I was about to witness one of them skirmishes I'd been hearing about. But truth to tell, I didn't have the stomach for it. Instead of watching those men kill each other, I pressed myself flat against the cold ground and shut my eyes. But I couldn't stop my ears from hearing the cries and screams.

I don't know how long the shooting went on—probably not near as long as it seemed—but when the gunfire stopped, I was scared to raise my head. I could hear Yankee voices, so I figured things had gone bad for the lieutenant and his men, which was a pity. He'd seemed a decent enough fellow.

"We got three wounded rebels. What do we do with them?" a Yankee hollered.

"Tie 'em up and bring 'em with us," the leader answered.

"How about the dead?"

"Bring ours. Leave theirs. We ain't got time to be burying any rebels."

"How about the slave women?"

I opened my eyes then and saw the Yankees had captured Maror, Hyacinth, and Pearl. The baby was wailing now, its reedy little voice rising above the moans and groans of the wounded men.

"Take 'em along." The leader swung into his saddle and headed downstream.

For once neither Maror nor Hyacinth had anything to say. They allowed the soldiers to hoist them on their horses and carry them away. I reckoned they were a heap better off with the Yankees than they would have been with the colonel and Mr. Cornelius Baxter. Most likely they thought so too.

From my hiding place, I saw the last of the Yankees ride back into the woods. On the ground near me lay four dead men. One of them was Mr. Baxter, flat on his back, a look of surprise on his face.

Near him lay the lieutenant. It made my heart ache to see him there. He wasn't very old, I thought, and I wondered if he'd lied to the army about his age, like Private Otis Hicks.

The flies had already found his wounds, and they was swarming all over the blood. I waved them away, and they rose in a buzzing cloud, as ugly as Beelzebub himself. But they didn't go away. They just hung in the air over Lieutenant Colston, biding their time. As soon as I quit disturbing them, they'd go back to their feast.

Sick to my stomach, I turned my head and threw up the little food left in my belly. What I'd seen on Pratt Street was nothing compared to this.

Since I couldn't do anything for them, I left the dead men behind and followed the river downstream. I walked slow, keeping my eye out for Perry. I hoped I'd find him somewhere along the way—lost in the woods, maybe.

As I trudged along, I called his name over and over. But he never answered. A crow cawed from the top of a dead tree. Gnats hummed and buzzed around my ears. Birds sang all around me just as if it was an ordinary day. To them I supposed it was. What men done to each other had no meaning for birds or beasts.

The longer I walked, the more sure I was I'd never see Perry again. All we'd been through was for nothing. He was most likely drowned and gone forever. I stumbled along, pretty near blind with tears.

Which is why I didn't see Colonel Abednego Botfield until it was too late. All of a sudden, he stepped out from behind a tree and grabbed me just as Lydia once had. But this time, there was a gun to my head instead of a knife at my throat. And I knew I'd found my death at last.

CHAPTER 16

Damned if it ain't Jesse Sherman, the plague of my life," the colonel muttered. "Seems I can't get away from you, boy." He looked and sounded bad, ashy-faced, his shirt and jacket all bloody, his voice low and hoarse. But his grip was as strong as ever.

"I seen you back there by the river." I spoke up as bold as I could, for nothing I said or did would make any difference now. "Riding away from the gunfire like some yellow dog."

"Fool horse threw me," the colonel said, letting fly a string of curses. "As for your yellow dogs," he went on with a smirk, "I figure it's better to be a living dog than a dead lion."

"Don't you go quoting the Bible to me, you old devil." Though my mouth was dry with fear, I managed to spit on the ground.

"Better show me some respect, Jesse Sherman." The colonel pressed his gun harder against my head. "You know what a bullet does to a boy's brain?"

I winced, for the muzzle of that revolver was cold and hard, and I could pretty well picture what a gunshot would do to me.

"Now," he said, "it seems to me if you're here, your little friend can't be far away. Why don't you quit playing and tell me where Lydia's boy is?"

"Even if I knew—which I don't—do you think I'd tell you?" I braced myself, expecting him to pull the trigger for sure.

Colonel Botfield was sagging a little, I thought, and growing more ashy faced, but he didn't loosen his grip on me or let his pistol waver. "You think I mean to harm him, don't you?"

"If you was to get Perry, I reckon you'd give him to the widow, like you done before. She just about killed him back in Baltimore. No doubt she'd relish the chance to finish what she started."

"Ah, Jesse, Jesse, you're such an ignorant boy. Philemon hasn't taught you enough to come in from the rain, has he?" The colonel gave a sharp laugh that turned into cough.

I was beginning to think he was hurt worse than I'd thought.

"Let's sit for a spell." Still keeping his gun on me, the colonel lowered himself to the ground and leaned against a tree. "Don't try running off. I'd just as soon shoot you as look at you. Besides, I got something to tell you. You wouldn't deny a fellow his deathbed confession, would you?"

"I don't want to hear none of your stories," I said, "whether you're dying or not. The sooner you take your last breath, the better, if you want to know."

"Seems you got no choice." The colonel waved his gun at me. "So listen up, boy. If you saw me ride away from the skirmish back there, I reckon you heard what transpired between me and Susie."

"Maror," I muttered, full of disgust for the man. "Her name is Maror."

"Not when I knew her," the colonel said. "She was Susanna then. Susie to me. Almighty young and pretty she was. And full of fire."

He stopped on account he was coughing. I thought maybe I could get away, but the second I moved, he grabbed hold of me.

When the coughing spell passed, Colonel Botfield said, "I'm not finished my story yet. I got myself a child by Susie. A daughter. You know who she was, don't you? Or are you even dumber than I think?"

I stared hard at the ground, counting each stone that lay there. Though I didn't say her name, the colonel grinned. "That's right. Lydia was my daughter."

I was so full of hate I could hardly speak. "You hunted your own kin. If you'd found her, you would've took the reward from the Widow Baxter and then sold Lydia south!"

"I'd have made sure she went somewhere good," the colonel protested. "Her and the boy both. In fact, I was making plans to send them to a friend of mine in Round Hill, the very same man I sold Susie to. Wouldn't she have been glad to see her mama again?"

The old devil spoke so proud you'd have thought he was a godly man doing the Lord's work, instead of the low villain he in fact was. He coughed again, long and hard. When he wiped his mouth, I saw blood. Once more I edged away, and once more he grabbed me.

"Trouble is, things didn't work out the way I planned, did they? First Lydia up and died having another baby by that fool Peregrine. Then you went and stuck your big nose into my affairs and made off with my grandson. I got him back, but I didn't count on my niece Henrietta being so vengeful."

He paused and looked at me hard. "So here I am, about to die in the woods with no one nearby but the most useless boy in the state of Maryland. I ask you, Jesse, what am I to do now?"

I shook my head, signifying I had no idea how to answer his question. Truth to tell, I neither knew nor cared what the villain did as long as he died without Perry knowing who his granddaddy was.

Colonel Botfield tightened his hold on my arm and stared into my eyes. "Promise me something," he whispered.

I drew back as far as I could, for I didn't want to

make no more promises to the dead. But that man's grip was like death itself. There was no escaping it.

"Find Perry," he said, "make sure he's safe. Don't care where. Slave or free. Give him the money I got in my pockets. Keep five dollars for my burial money and see it's done proper. Don't let me rot in the woods like an animal."

He stopped to cough. "Keep going along the river the way you were and you'll come to the ferry. Should be someone there willing to fetch my body."

I watched the colonel sag back against the tree trunk. He was breathing hard, working to get air. I knew from the raspy sound he was making he didn't have long in this world.

"Promise me you'll do all I said," he mumbled, fixing me with that stare of his. "And tell Perry who gave him the money. He ought to know. I never meant him no harm. Nor Lydia either."

No matter how pitiful the man was now, he'd done a heap of harm to many a slave, including Lydia and Perry. I fought to harden my heart against him, but pity got the best of me. I ended up giving him my word, thus binding myself to yet another promise.

Colonel Botfield lingered a while, more dead than alive. He didn't open his eyes, nor did he speak again. I could have gone off and left him, but he was as fearful of dying alone as any man. So I sat with him and watched and waited.

With some agony, Colonel Abednego Botfield

finally passed from this world to the next. There wasn't nothing peaceful about his going or the expression on his face. The old villain looked as fierce as if he'd died in sight of hell's gates. Which no doubt he had.

I sat there a while, staring at the corpse. He was the first man I'd seen die right before my very eyes. Alive and full of evil one second, dead and empty the next. Where was the colonel's soul now?

If there was any justice, I reckoned he was burning in the fiery furnace. Unlike his namesake in the Bible story, Colonel Abednego Botfield didn't have the company of Shadrach and Meshach. Nor was he going to step out of the flames unhurt like those three. Surely God would not take pity on that villain's soul.

It took a while to get the courage to reach into the pockets of the colonel's coat and fish out a leather bag. Inside I found close to three hundred dollars in gold coins, as well as enough silver to pay the burial expenses. It was more money than I'd seen in my entire life. If I ever found Perry, he'd be a wealthy boy.

I got to my feet and looked down at my old enemy. "When I get to the ferry landing," I promised, "I'll tell someone where you are. I'll make sure they know your name and where you come from. You'll get your proper burial, colonel."

I hesitated a moment. "And I'll do my best to find Perry and give him the money. I'll tell him who gave it to him, too."

With that, I turned my back on Colonel Abednego Botfield and continued along the river toward New Berlin, still hoping to meet Perry somewhere up ahead.

———————————

I reached the ferry landing sometime in the afternoon. The sun had finally broke through the clouds, and the Potomac river shone like silver. The ferry had just come across, and I went up to a kindly looking man in the crowd.

"I don't know if you heard," I said, "but there was a skirmish up the river a ways. The Yankees left the Confederate dead lying where they fell. Mr. Cornelius Baxter was one of them."

"Cornelius Baxter?" The man studied me as if he suspected me of funning him. "I saw him just a few days ago crossing this very river, and now you say he's dead?"

I nodded, and the fellow with him said, "I don't know nothing about who was killed, but the boy's right about the skirmish. A lot of folks heard the gunfire."

Another man nodded, his round face solemn. "They say the Yankees rounded up some runaway slaves—women and children, a man, too. Don't intend to return them either. They're keeping them as contraband."

A big bubble of hope swelled in my chest, but I kept

my face plain. Didn't even smile. "Was one of them a boy about yea high? Light-complected?"

The man shrugged and spit in the gutter. "I didn't see them myself. Don't know what they looked like. Don't care neither."

I figured I'd better drop the subject of runaways before the men got suspicious of me. Didn't want them thinking I was a Yankee eager to aid and abet. Though, truth to tell, I guessed I was.

"Farther down the river, closer to town," I went on, "I come across Colonel Abednego Botfield from Talbot County, Maryland. Shot by the Yankees. Before he died, he gave me some money to see he was buried proper."

I paused and gazed at the men. "Can one of you gentlemen fetch the colonel's body and tend to the matter?"

"I know Abednego," the first man said, pulling a long face. "I'm grieved to hear of his death. I'll make certain his remains are shipped back to Talbot County."

Though it surprised me to hear anyone admit to grieving for the colonel, I handed him some silver. "I'm almighty grateful to you, sir. A promise to a dying man—"

"Don't worry yourself, boy," the man cut in. "Things will be done proper for Abednego. He was a good man, true to the Cause."

He tipped his hat and strolled away with his friends,

talking low and sorrowful. They shook their heads and cussed Mr. Abraham Lincoln for causing all this grief and woe.

After I boarded the ferry, I saw the men assembling wagons and horses to go and gather the dead. I breathed a deep sigh, for I'd fulfilled one part of my promise to Colonel Abednego Botfield. All I had to do now was find Perry and do the rest.

CHAPTER 17

The ferry docked in New Berlin late in the afternoon. Despite the sunshine, the breeze had a chilly nip, and I was cold and weary and hungry. I headed uphill into town, wishing I could use some of Perry's money for food, but I was pretty sure I'd be hauled off to jail if I tried. Where would an ignorant boy such as myself have gotten a silver coin?

When I saw a man come walking toward me, I stepped in front of him. "Pardon me, sir, but do you know where the Yankee camp is?"

He regarded me with humorous contempt. "Which one? There must be dozens of bluebellies infesting the woods around here."

"I was hoping to find the ones that snuck across the river this morning and skirmished with the rebels."

"Oh, that must be Captain Granger's boys." He

pointed at the hills around us. "Just go on up there and start asking. You'll find them sooner or later."

With that he strolled into a tavern, leaving me to begin my search. I trudged through the woods for a long ways, staggering with weariness and hunger. The bag of money clinked in my pocket, getting heavier with each step. I guess the jingle of the coins put me in mind of the colonel, for I kept looking behind me, expecting to see the old devil riding after me on that big bay horse of his. I knew he was dead, but I swear his ghost scared me even more than the living man.

At every camp I was met with suspicion and questions. No one knew the whereabouts of Captain Granger. No one cared. But they sure wondered why I was wanting to know. I asked once or twice for Private Otis Hicks, thinking he'd put in a good word for me, but nobody had ever heard of him.

Finally a guard told me I'd come to the right camp at last. "What do you want with the captain?" he asked.

"There was a skirmish this morning, just across the river," I said. "I hear his men brought some slaves back with them."

"What's it to you if they did?" He eyed me with scorn. "Those slaves are contraband now."

I longed to punch that soldier as hard as I could, but I knew such a deed wouldn't advance my cause. Forcing myself to speak civil, I said, "Can you at least tell me if there was a boy with them? A pretty child about seven years old?"

The guard grinned. "You have anything to make my telling you worthwhile?"

I reached into my pocket and brought out some silver coins. "This is all I got."

The guard counted the money. "Fifty cents. I reckon that's enough to stake me to a game of cards tonight."

Dropping the coins into his pocket, he said, "There was a boy, three women, a baby, and a man. The last I seen of 'em, they was near the hospital tent." He pointed off to the left. "Seems the man was wounded."

It was the best use I could have put that money to. I thanked the Yankee and ran off, hoping to find Perry fast. It took longer than I reckoned, though. Almost every soldier I passed stopped me and asked where I was going and what I was doing. Luckily they all thought I was way too young to be a danger to anyone. By the time I found the hospital tent I was weary of their questions and their jokes, which all seemed to be at my expense.

The first person I saw was Hyacinth. She was standing with her back to me, gazing through the trees at the setting sun. The clouds had turned to purple and deep red, and the sky itself was like a lake of fire.

I went up to her quiet-like and said her name.

She wheeled around, amazed to see me. "Jesse," she whispered, "we never thought to see you again, boy. Where have you been?"

"Trying to catch up with you." I grabbed her hand. "Where's Perry? Is he all right?"

"Bless you, Perry's fine, but worried sick about you." She led me toward a small tent. "He's going to be real happy to see you, Jesse."

Hyacinth lifted the flap and led me inside. "Look who I just found," she cried.

Perry let out a squeal and ran to me. The two of us hugged each other so hard we nearly squeezed the breath out of ourselves. When we let loose, Maror gave me a hug herself. Pearl was sitting beside Thomas. He sported a bandage on his head and a sling on his arm but appeared to be in no danger of dying. They greeted me with smiles, and the baby whimpered.

"Sit yourself down and have something to eat," Hyacinth said. "Poor thing, you look half starved."

I took a plate of beans and dug in. They were hot and tasty, full of salt and pork fat. I grinned at Perry, and he grinned back. Truth to tell, I felt like I'd been reunited with my own family, the one I'd never had and always wanted.

After I'd eaten my full, I told them what had transpired, leaving out nothing but the colonel's last words and the bag of money. I planned to wait until Perry and I were alone to give him his inheritance, for I still hadn't decided exactly what to tell him.

Maror gave me a grim smile. "That's the best news I've heard in a long while," she muttered. "I just wish I'd been the one to shoot the devil."

Hyacinth patted her mother's hand. "Forget Colonel Abednego Botfield, Mama. Put him behind you, along with your old name." She glanced at Perry, who was too busy toying with a loose button on his jacket to notice. "That man can't harm you or anyone else now."

Not caring to linger on this subject, I turned my attention to Thomas. "What happened after I got swept away from the boat? Where were you and Perry all that time?"

Thomas shrugged. "A bullet hit my arm and another grazed my head. Since I wasn't no use the way I was, I went overboard with Perry. We got washed down the river a way and hid ourselves amongst the rocks. The soldiers found us and took us along with the women."

"We'd have stayed to look for you, Jesse," Maror put in, "but the Yankees were in a rush to get back across the river."

"What do you aim to do now?" I asked. "The camp guard said you're contraband. Does that mean you're prisoners?"

Thomas shook his head. "I told the captain we was on our way to Ohio, and he said to go on with his blessings. What would they want with us? We're just more mouths to feed."

"We'll be leaving first thing tomorrow," Maror said. "Before the sun's up. War or no war, we've still got danger to face."

"Are you coming with us, Jesse?" Perry asked.

I was sore tempted to say yes. But if I ran off to Ohio, who would care for Uncle Philemon? It worried me not to be there to hunt his dinner. The Lord only knew what he'd been eating all this time. Living on biscuits and eggs, most like, and whatever else Delia could concoct.

"I wish I could go with you, but I reckon I'd best go on home," I said slowly. "My uncle's a cussed old critter sometimes, but he needs me to look after him."

Perry's lip jutted out like he was fixing to cry, but the others nodded as if they understood. It occurred to me they might not want a white boy tagging along with them. What would I be but an everlasting reminder of their old life? It distressed me to think such thoughts but, like it or not, a person has to face facts every now and then.

Seeing how upset Perry was, I asked Maror if it was all right for him and me to take a walk together.

"Stay close by," she said. "I don't want some Yankee taking potshots at you."

Once we were by ourselves, Perry wouldn't talk. He acted just like he used to, sulking and pouting and refusing to look at me. Finally I got fed up, the same as I always did.

"Listen here, Perry," I said. "I got important things to tell you, and this is my last chance to do it. You sit down on that there stone and listen."

Took by surprise, Perry did as I asked. I pulled the

bag of money out of my pocket, glad to rid myself of its weight, and dangled it in front of him. "You see this?"

"'Course I do," Perry said, as sassy as ever. "I'm not blind, you know."

"Well, there's almost three hundred dollars' worth of gold coins here, and it's all yours." I dropped the bag in his lap.

Perry picked it up and felt its heft. Then he peeked inside as if he suspicioned he'd find rocks. His eyes widened when he saw the gold coins. "Where did you get this, Jesse?"

"From your grandpa," I said.

"Judge Baxter?" he asked.

"You know of any other grandpa you might have?"

Perry shook his head. "But where did you see him? I thought he was in Baltimore." The suspicious look came back.

"Well, as I was waiting for the ferry, who did I see but Miss Polly and the judge. I reckon Baltimore was no longer to the judge's liking—all them Yankees making life hard for him. Anyway, he come right up to me and asked where you were. I told him I hoped to find you at a Yankee camp across the river."

I paused to see how Perry was taking my lie. I'd been thinking it up ever since I'd left the colonel. As far as I could tell, I'd done what the villain asked. I'd told Perry the money was from his grandpa, and that was the truth.

"And then the judge gave you this?" Perry lifted the pouch.

"That's just what your grandpa did. I reckon he must have felt bad about not doing anything for you before."

Perry opened the bag again and took out one of the coins. He studied it a while and then put it back. "Let's go tell Grandmother and Aunt Hyacinth," he said. "Won't they be happy?"

Perry ran toward the tent, and I followed him, my heart heavier than the bag of gold. It was one thing for Perry to believe my story, but I was pretty sure Maror and Hyacinth would see the holes in it.

I stood back and watched Perry give his granny the money. As she took it, she shot me a look full of questions. The first chance she had, she took me aside. Making sure Perry was busy playing with Pearl's baby, she said, "No more stories, Jesse. What did Abednego tell you before he gave you that money?"

She'd figured it out even faster than I thought she would. So even though I was worried of hurting her in some way, I told her the truth. "The colonel said he was Lydia's daddy and Perry was his grandson, and that I was to give the money in his pocket to Perry and tell him who it come from. Which I did." I raised my eyes to hers. "It ain't my fault the only granddaddy Perry knows is Judge Baxter."

"You have more sense than I thought," Maror said softly. Turning her head, she watched Perry for a few seconds. When she looked at me again, her face was full of sorrow. "I pray that child never learns he's kin to the colonel. Much as I loved Lydia, I didn't choose that man to be her father. I fought him as hard as I could, but he was stronger than I was. That's the truth of it."

I understood what she was saying, and it made me hate Colonel Abednego Botfield more than ever.

"I did my best to convince Lydia not to let a white man take her the way the colonel took me," Maror went on, "but she was so sure Peregrine was a good man. I reckon he was, up to a point. But he didn't have any qualms about sending Hyacinth and me away, did he?"

Maror paused and looked at me hard. "Lord," she said, "listen to me talking to you like you're a grown man instead of a boy. I don't know what came over me."

She got to her feet and went to Perry. "Come along, child," she said softly. "It's time to get some rest." Turning to me, she added, "You lie down, too, Jesse. You've had a mighty long day."

I lay down beside Perry, and Maror covered us with a Union army blanket made of the scratchiest, smelliest wool ever spun from a sheep's back.

"I wish you were coming with us," Perry whispered. "I'm going to miss you awful bad."

"I'll miss you, too, Perry."

"Maybe you can come visiting after we get settled," Perry murmured. "Maybe we can . . ." His voice trailed off in a drowsy murmur, and he fell sound asleep.

I was mighty tired myself, but I didn't fall asleep right away. I lay still and watched the others bed down, Maror and Hyacinth sharing one blanket, and Thomas, Pearl, and the baby sharing another. I listened to them talking, their voices too low for me to catch their words. It was a soothing sound, soft and comfortable.

Outside the tent, soldiers moved around, talking and laughing, cussing each other every now and then in a mostly good-natured way. A horse whinnied somewhere. A man hollered. The wind tugged at the canvas walls of the tent, making a creaking sound like sails on a boat.

For some reason, I felt safer than I had since I'd left the Shore, maybe because the colonel was dead. I didn't need to fear him nor his ghost, for I'd kept my promise to him.

But at the same time, I was sad, for this was the last night I'd spend with Perry. Tomorrow he'd be on his way to his new home, and I'd be on my way to my old home. Most likely I'd never see him or Maror or Hyacinth again. Though it shames me to admit it, I pressed my face into that smelly old army blanket and cried myself to sleep.

CHAPTER 18

The next day I said my good-byes, though it nearly broke my heart to do it. Thomas and Pearl went on ahead, but Hyacinth and Maror lingered a while to give Perry and me a little more time together.

"You won't forget to mark Mama's grave?" Perry asked.

I shook my head, only slightly riled he'd ask such a question. "It's the first thing I aim to do."

Perry stuck out his hand, and I shook it. "Thank you for bringing me here, Jesse," he said. "I hope to see you again sometime."

Tears rose up in his eyes, and he turned his head to wipe them away. I was close to crying myself.

Maror took Perry's hand. "It's time to go. We have a long journey ahead of us."

"You be careful now," I told him. "I don't want to

hear nothing about slave catchers when I come out to Ohio for my visit."

With a heavy heart, I watched Perry walk away, Maror on one side and Hyacinth on the other. Several times he turned and waved, and I waved back. At a curve in the road, Perry waved one last time, and then he was gone. There was nothing for me to do but turn my back on the mountains and begin my long journey home.

I don't know how many miles I walked, getting a ride every now and then in some kind soul's wagon. I lost track of the days, too, but I can tell you they were long and hot. Or long and rainy. Don't know which was worse. But I wore the soles of my shoes clear through long before I got to Baltimore.

From time to time I ran into a bunch of Federals on patrol. I soon learned to hide when I saw them coming, for they always questioned me as if they suspicioned I was a spy for the South. Sometimes they made sport of me, teasing and threatening to put me in jail, roughing me up, boxing my ears and such. Once they took the only food I had, a loaf of bread an old lady had given me.

The Confederates were just as bad. The one time I met up with some of them, they wanted to draft me on the spot. Or kill me for fear I'd tell the Yankees I'd seen them. I was lucky to escape with my life.

By the time I reached Baltimore, I was surprised to see even more soldiers than before. The city was crawling with bluebellies as thick as ticks on a hound dog. But they paid no mind to me. In Baltimore I was just another barefoot boy, of no danger to anyone.

I made my way to the harbor and began searching for Captain Harrison. It took me a long while to find him, but I finally spotted him on the dock, overseeing the sale of his catch. When he saw me coming, I swear he turned pale.

"Jesse, is that you in the flesh?" he asked.

I stretched out my hand, and he took it real cautious-like. When he felt the solid flesh, he drew me close and hugged me, filling my nose with the good smell of fish.

"We'd given you up for dead, boy!" he cried. "You and that little child both."

"No, sir, we're both living still," I said. "It's Colonel Abednego Botfield that's dead, not Perry nor me."

While the crew readied the *Sally H.* to sail home, I told the captain all that had happened since I'd said good-bye to him that day in April. He interrupted me every now and then to praise the Lord. When I was done talking, he shared his dinner of cheese and bread with me.

"Your uncle will be mighty pleased to see you alive and well," Captain Harrison said, "but I got to warn you, he's doing poorly hisself. He took a chill hunting turtles last month, and he's been ailing ever since. Miss Sally's done her best with poultices and such, but he don't seem to improve."

It was just as I feared. Without me to do the hunting and fishing, Uncle Philemon had got himself into a sorry state. "He ain't fixing to die, is he?"

Captain Harrison gave me a glum look. "It just might be the sight of you will perk him up some."

So instead of enjoying the journey down the Bay, I stood at the rail and worried about my uncle. As the shoreline slid past, I couldn't help thinking about the colonel as well. I'd been running from him for such a long time I could hardly believe the old villain was really and truly dead. What if those men I'd sent to fetch his body found him alive after all? Why, at this very moment he could be coming after me on a big steam boat, wanting his money back, wanting Perry, wanting the devil knew what. Hadn't Colonel Abednego Botfield said he'd be the death of me? And yet it hadn't happened that way. He was dead, and I was alive.

But still—what if the colonel's ghost came to me? I'd done what he asked but not the way he'd wished. Despite the hot sunshine, I shivered and looked over my shoulder. All I saw was Daniel Wrightson mopping the deck, his shadow moving slow and natural as he worked.

When the *Sally H.* docked, I was the first ashore. I thanked Captain Harrison and ran for home, scarcely feeling the crushed oyster shells cutting my bare feet. Couldn't help glancing behind me every now and then, but there was neither horse nor man following after me, just the empty road striped with shadows from the afternoon sun.

The old house was as tumbledown as ever, but I sure was happy it was still standing. Delia saw me coming and ran to meet me. Though I hoped for a big smile, all I got was a scolding and a box on my ears for being gone so long.

"We gave you up for dead months ago," she cried. "What caused you to run off like that, with no word to anyone? Why, we even had dogs searching the marsh for your body."

Delia dragged me into the house, fussing every step of the way. "And your uncle almost dead himself," she cried. "How come you to be so ungrateful and me thinking you was a good boy!"

When she finally stopped shaking me and hollering in my face, I told her about Lydia and Perry and Maror and all that had happened since that day in April. It took a while to get the story out for she kept asking questions, but when I was done talking, she hugged me and busted out crying for joy and sorrow both. Joy that Maror was safe along with Perry and Hyacinth. Sorrow that Lydia wasn't with them.

Wiping her eyes and blowing her nose, Delia said, "Oh, my Lord, Jesse, I plumb forgot about Mr. Philemon. You get on upstairs and see the poor man. He's missed you something terrible."

I ran up the steps two at a time and flung open the door to Uncle Philemon's room. The old fellow was lying in bed, propped up on his pillows, snoring away the afternoon. I went up to him and touched his shoulder.

He was so startled to wake up and see me, he

hollered out loud and then started into coughing like he'd never stop, all the while staring at me like I was the angel of death, come to take him across the river Jordan.

"It's just me—Jesse," I said. "As you can see, I ain't dead after all."

Uncle Philemon took a drink of whiskey and stopped coughing. "Where the devil have you been all this time, boy?"

"I'm sorry I was gone so long, Uncle Philemon, but, truth to tell, I got into some trouble." I hesitated for I wasn't sure what to say next, knowing his feelings about aiding and abetting and such.

"I reckon it had something to do with that little slave child Abednego Botfield wanted so bad," Uncle Philemon said.

I stared at him, surprised. "How did you know about Perry?"

"Oh, Miss Sally Harrison dropped a few hints when she was treating me for the pneumonia. She believed I was dying and hoped to put my mind at ease about you. Running off to Baltimore with a fugitive slave. What a damn fool thing for you to do." Uncle Philemon coughed and took another sip of whiskey. "I figured Abednego had most likely murdered you. A man like him don't stop at nothing to rid his self of enemies."

"The colonel done his best to kill me," I said, "but it may surprise you to know it's him that's dead, not me."

Uncle Philemon nodded as if I was telling him old

news. "Seems Abednego's corpse got home before you did. The rascal's been in the ground for almost a month, I reckon, buried nice and proper in St. Michael's churchyard." He poured another glass of whiskey and lifted it like a toast. "Well, God speed the man's soul to perdition, I say. Now I don't have to pay him the money I owed him from our last card game."

"Hear, hear," I said, joining the toast without having a drop to drink. Nothing could have pleased me more than knowing the colonel was truly in his grave, all promises kept and no reason to haunt me.

Uncle Philemon reached for my hand. "I must say I missed you, Jesse, and I'm glad you're home, even though I fear you picked up some Yankee notions while you was gone. You know how I feel about aiding and abetting. If I was well, I'd give you a good thrashing."

He lay back and closed his eyes. "But I ain't well and I need my nap, so you run along now and make yourself useful. Hunt me up a turtle or something. I ain't had a decent meal since you left."

I did as my uncle said and went on downstairs. It didn't seem worthwhile to start preaching at him about what I'd learned in my travels with Perry. The old man was set in his ways now and not about to change his views.

The very next morning I went down to the marsh and caught the biggest turtle in all of Talbot County. Delia made the finest soup ever concocted, and a few days later Uncle Philemon rose from his bed, feeling almost like his old self. He took a seat on the veranda and set me to work hammering and nailing whilst he sipped whiskey. It seemed many things had fallen apart in my absence.

"This is your chance to learn the art of carpentry," Uncle Philemon told me, "A fine and useful trade."

The first chance I had, I used my newfound skills to fashion a cross from hardwood. When it was done, I carved Lydia's name and dates deep so the letters and numbers wouldn't wear away. If Uncle Philemon knew what I was making, he didn't say a word. In fact, he never spoke of Lydia nor the colonel nor my Yankee ways again.

One fine July morning, I walked through the marsh to the place in the woods where she lay waiting.

I pounded the cross into the ground, and then I knelt down and read the words out loud to her. "Here lies Liddia, deerly beluved mama of Perry, and her baby girl. Died 1861. Rest in Peece."

I was silent a minute or two. The sun shone through the leaves, burning hot, and gnats buzzed around my face. The earth had sunk some where Lydia was buried, and moss had started growing, a nice green cover for her and the baby. Birds sang like a church choir, and I felt sad but peaceful.

"I done my best to keep my promise to you," I told Lydia. "Perry's with your mama and sister now, living free in Ohio. I know you wanted him to stay with Polly

Baxter, but she wasn't much use. I hope you won't blame me none for not doing exactly what you asked."

I swear I heard Lydia's voice saying I did well, though I guess it must have been the leaves murmuring in the breeze.

"Another thing," I added, "Colonel Abednego Botfield is dead, so he won't be chasing Perry ever again."

Those leaves fluttered like they was laughing.

"I just wish you was in Ohio with Perry," I told her, "not lying here in these dark woods."

Once again the breeze ruffled the leaves, splashing sunlight in my eyes. I laid a handful of wildflowers on the grave and got to my feet. Then I walked slowly home. There was still plenty of work waiting for me.

AFTERWORD

Promises to the Dead began as most of my books do—with a vision. I saw a boy in a marsh on a rainy day long ago, hunting turtles for his uncle. As I pondered the story he was no doubt a part of, I saw him again—this time in a dark woods, captured by a runaway slave. As a result of that encounter, Jesse leaves his home on Maryland's Eastern Shore and journeys first to Baltimore and then to northern Virginia across the Potomac River from what is now Brunswick, Maryland.

In the spring of 1861, Maryland was a slave-holding state with a strong inclination to secede from the Union. The Eastern Shore and the city of Baltimore were particularly loyal to the southern cause. Indeed, had not the federal government intervened, Maryland would most likely have joined the Confederacy.

The Pratt Street Riot on April 19, 1861 was

Baltimore's response to President Lincoln's effort to squelch the rebellion begun in South Carolina on April 12, 1861. On April 13, Major Robert Anderson, Union Army, surrendered Fort Sumter to Confederate General Pierre Gustave Toutant Beauregard. The federal fort had been under fire by southern troops for thirty-four hours; in all that time no one on either side had been killed.

Determined to regain Fort Sumter, President Abraham Lincoln called for an army of 75,000 volunteers. Thousands of men responded immediately to the president's call. To reach the South, these troops had to pass through Baltimore.

Four companies of the 25th Pennsylvania Volunteers arrived at Bolton Station on April 18, 1861. At that time, Baltimore prohibited locomotives from pulling trains through the city. To continue their journey south, the soldiers had to make their way on foot to the Camden Street Station. When they left the train cars, a mob assembled and hurled bricks and paving stones at them. Nicholas Biddle, a Union officer's black servant, was killed in the melee. He is often described as the first casualty of the Civil War.

Unfortunately, the events of April 18 were merely a warmup for what happened the next day. On April 19, the Massachusetts Militia arrived at the President Street Station, near Fells Point. They, too, had to go through the city to reach Camden Street Station, but unlike the Pennsylvania Volunteers, they were transported from one station to the other in railroad cars pulled by horses along Pratt Street. The soldiers were armed but had been told not to shoot unless they were fired upon.

The first seven units reached Camden Street Station safely, but a large mob attacked the Massachusetts companies at the end of the line, as well as an unarmed regimental band from New York and a unit of Pennsylvania Volunteers. The rioters dumped cartloads of sand on the tracks. They hauled anchors from nearby piers and threw them in front of the horses, blocking the train cars. Joining the melee, citizens pelted the soldiers with rocks, bricks, bottles, and anything else they could throw.

Soon the riot on Pratt Street turned into a battle. Civilians fired on the soldiers, and the soldiers fired back.

At that point, Mayor George W. Brown placed himself at the head of the soldiers' column and marched beside their commanding officer. Marshal George P. Kane and a squad of Baltimore police formed a line in the rear of troops.

When the battle ended—the first of the Civil War, some say—four soldiers had been killed and thirty-six wounded. Twelve Baltimore citizens were killed and an unknown number wounded.

To prevent further incidents, General Benjamin Franklin Butler made a decision. On the night of May 13, 1861, he led five hundred men from the 6th Massachusetts, veterans of the Pratt Street Riot, into Baltimore under cover of a thunderstorm. The troops occupied Federal Hill above the harbor. While the city slept, Butler's men set up guns and aimed them down Charles Street, straight at the Washington Monument in Mount Vernon Place. Any more trouble and the good folks of Baltimore would find their city under fire.

Butler acted on his own initiative and, for that reason, was later relieved of his command. However, Baltimore remained under martial law for the duration of the war, and Maryland remained in the Union, a state of strategic importance despite its small size.

Many Marylanders continued to be sympathetic to the South. Numbers of young men fled to Virginia and joined the Confederate army, later fighting against their fellow Marylanders at Front Royal and Gettysburg. Some of their fathers were jailed at Fort McHenry for treason against the Union. Like Uncle Philemon, most of them claimed to be opposed to the federal government's encroachment on states' rights.

Other young men heeded Lincoln's call in even greater numbers, forming the Maryland Volunteer Infantry in May 1861.

Although the Emancipation Proclamation freed slaves in Confederate states, it did not free the slaves in Maryland, a Union state. As late as July 1863, three weeks after the Battle of Gettysburg, Union officers liberated the inmates of a slave trader's jail near the Baltimore harbor.

This is the Baltimore in which Jesse and Perry find themselves when they arrive on April 19, 1861. "Mob

Town" it was called then—and for good reason. With the exception of their encounter with Colonel Abednego Botfield, the events the boys experience really happened in pretty much the way Jesse describes them.

Later in the story, when Jesse witnesses a "Baltimore Belle" mocking a Union soldier, he is actually seeing my great-grandparents on the day they met—one for the South and one for the North, like so many Baltimoreans.